Polimony

A. B. Lawrence

This is a work of fiction. Similarities to real people, places, or events are entirely coincidental.

POLIMONY

First edition. December 3rd, 2024.

Copyright © 2024 A.B. Lawrence

Written by: A.B. Lawrence

Table of Contents

ACT I

I

Everybody needs somebody. So, I have Polimony.

She never told me her name. I'd never thought to ask. It was one of those axiomatic things on which everything else laid. Like basic arithmetic, light and dark, Polimony.

Polimony doesn't go anywhere without me, so she doesn't get out much. Not that she appears to mind. It would seem that we make up for our distrust in others with our full trust in one another. Some might say that's kind of pathetic, having an imaginary friend.

That's why I consider her a muse instead. There's something more adult about that.

...

Simon, wake up!

Another dream ruined by Polimony. When I opened my eyes all I could see were a separate set of blue ones staring back.

Don't look at me like I interrupted something. Today is the day you finally do something.

That smug look. That teasing voice. No, too early for any of it. I squeezed my eyes shut and rolled over.

What are you doing? Wake up! It'll be a different dream this time anyway.

I could hardly remember what the dream was about, but that didn't matter.

"Go away, I don't want to wake up to this! I was sleeping off this hangover in peace!" I tried to nudge her off me with absolutely no success.

You've got to be kidding me. You can be so pathetic.

I sprang out of bed and forced a laugh. "Pathetic? I'm a visionary"

You're right, pathetic was the wrong word. You're unemployed.

A smile formed beneath my tired eyes. "'I can be so unemployed?' That doesn't make any sense."

I'm leaving the room before you make me angry. I will see you in the kitchen.

I rolled my eyes as she dramatically stomped out. "I'm getting up, I just need to..."

The sentence was suspended, unfinished, in the oddly late feeling air. A glance out the window solved the mystery immediately. The spot in the sky where I had expected the sun to be was unoccupied. Instead, the sun was several hours west.

"Hmm."

My feet froze on the kitchen tiles as I started a pot of coffee. This section of living space matched much of the rest; it was small but had everything we needed plus a little bit more. A small island counter top, a compact wood dining set, and a custom backsplash tiled by me (with my muse's hesitant consent on the pattern). Polimony stood in the middle of the kitchen with her arms crossed, staring at the floor. Her silence could be worse than when she spoke.

The coffee maker awkwardly bubbled behind me.

"Oddly afternoon looking, this morning..." I smiled weakly at her, hoping my lame attempt at humor would lighten her mood. She looked up at me, visibly angry. I couldn't even breathe before she began.

That's because it's noon! Haha, I'm joking! It's four! PM! Go ahead, check!

I could take her word for it.

Oh wait! That's right, I shouldn't ask you to do anything yet. You haven't had anything to drink.

"This feels unnecessary."

No, what's unnecessary is taking this long to wake up, then immediately being mean to me.

"You were hovering over me!"

I thought you liked it when I hovered over you.

"You didn't do it the way that I liked," I shook my head and began aimlessly pacing the kitchen. "I'm not prepared for this level of action, this early in the morning."

Polimony pouted.

You're right, the world and I can wait until you've had yours.

"You're making my head hurt."

Is it the lack of caffeine? Is it a hangover? Or have you finally graduated to full blown alcoholism, and the withdrawal is slowly inching its way towards you?

"All of this nonsense sounds very familiar. Hmm. I wonder." My hand immediately made its way towards the liquor cabinet, conveniently located above the coffee maker. Polimony walked back into the bedroom shaking her head.

You're a real piece of shit.

"I don't know where you're going, I'm planning to head out soon."

Her voice echoed into the kitchen, *Are you going to creep on that girl again? You've still got an hour.*

"No! I have a mind to do something productive today."

Yeah. Right. Let me get dressed.

"Don't rush, I need to make this drink and then check the answering machine."

There was a stifled chuckle and then a second or so of silence. *Still holding out hope?*

"...She might've called, it is within the realm of reason that she has called."

To... get the rest of her stuff. And even that isn't within any 'realm of reason'. It isn't even within the 'realm of probability'. It's been months.

I frowned and bobbed my head to imaginary music, attempting to force out the memories that came to mind. Preparing a mixture of black coffee and gin, I shut my eyes and allowed the subtle scent of alcohol to tickle my nose. Inhale. Exhale. It always smells better than it tastes. I shuffled towards our answering machine and sipped, cringing as liquor met stomach acid in the middle of my throat. The plastic fossil had shut off again, forcing me to angrily unplug and plug it back in repeatedly. The little display came to life on the fourth try.

A laugh came from behind me, *Guess the fourth time was the charm.*

Today Polimony had put on a black coat, a white shirt, and a long gray skirt. Hardly anything stimulating, or remotely fashionable for that matter.

"When the third isn't, the fourth or fifth usually is."

There were several messages. Unfortunately, the more rational side of me knew that they were from Marcus. Not from Anna.

Polimony wrinkled her nose in response to my apparent disappointment.

Stop pretending it annoys you, he just wants to help.

"Is that what you call that? Helping? Not, 'Pestering' or 'Pleading'?"

You act like we're made of money. You should at least press play and hear him out.

"No. And I act like *I'm* made of money. What do *you* paint exactly?"

I could paint the wall with our blood. Do you think I would mind you walking with a limp for the rest of this life?

"That isn't very nice or funny..."

Just call him. He only wants to help.

Polimony flipped her hair and I dialed his cellphone number, placing the receiver to my ear as the other end began to ring.

"I'm not a charity case."

Yeah. And the bank accepts pride in place of money.

I held a finger to my lips as Marcus' lightly accented voice chirped through the earpiece.

"Simon, my friend. I'm glad you're finally... awake?"

I didn't have to see him to know he was sarcastically looking around, pretending he didn't know it was four in the afternoon, all for his own dramatic effect.

"Yeah, sorry. I couldn't get to sleep last night. Why'd you call?"

... Silence on the other end. He knew that I knew why.

I rapped my fingers on the counter top impatiently. "Hello?"

"...I'm still here *Simone*,"

I hated it when he said my name like that.

"Why must you lie and force me to teach you with my silence?"

So original.

"... Simon? Are you there?"

So dramatic.

"Yeah, I'm still here."

There was another moment of quiet, interrupted only by bits of background noise. He was in his shop.

"You need to creep out from under this funk of yours, my friend! There are still galleries that want their own *Anna*,"

That name made my insides itch. I tried not to think about my last piece. I tried even harder not to think of its subject matter.

"In fact, I have had several buyers ask about you in the past week. You are very hard to forget about! It doesn't even need to be a good piece! Just put something out here with your name on it, I won't even charge a high commission! We can talk about it? I hate to think you wallowing in your apartment."

Polimony's face grazed mine. I jumped up and glared at her.

How generous of him in our time of need!

"No, there's no need for any of that! As if I could forget my dear friend and commissioner! In fact, I've already begun a new project! I was calling to let you know is all."

I savored the surprised look that I imagined on Marcus' face as Polimony shook her head and walked away.

Marcus cleared his throat, "Is that right? Apologies, my friend, I hate to interrupt. There's no rush, I wanted to let you know that the market is ready. Always ready. And I am also ready to help."

"I'll be sure to keep that in mind! I'm very busy so I'll speak with you some other time, okay? Bye for now!"

I slammed the receiver into place before he could say anything else. Polimony had put on a look of disbelief.

New project?

A change of plans.

"Of course! I told you that today would be productive."

You didn't mean 'a long walk to the liquor store'?

"Only after I put this project in motion, this project that I have been thinking of putting in motion for quite some time now..."

I grabbed my coat and avoided making eye contact with my skeptical muse. She was right to suspect that I was lying again. I absolutely was.

Main Street was appropriately crowded given the time of day. It was the early afternoon: everyone young was on their way home, and everyone old was going out to eat. This was only one of many regularly scheduled movements of bodies. And so the veins of the city circulated, with a regular rhythm, everyday. Usually I found the predictability comforting but today it felt like everybody was just in the way. The cold December air slowly displaced that of Autumn. We wove through it, the quiet breeze getting tangled in trees before escaping with a leaf or two. It was that perfect period building up to the holidays, where the few leaves that still remained would endlessly drift down before crunching beneath our feet. Today I decided to catch the odd one, examining the color to judge whether to keep or discard it. Rich hues floated all around us: deep oranges, rich reds, smokey siennas and delicate yellows.

Polimony was right and, to a lesser extent, so was Marcus. I hadn't done anything for quite some time. Through my weaselly deception,

I had painted myself into a rather necessary corner. The only way out was to actually paint something. On the spot, I decided leaves would definitely be a part of that. In no time at all, I had a pocket full of vibrant, decaying, plant matter. Polimony clearly wasn't buying it, rolling her eyes at my emphasized inspections of each leaf. Still, she walked silently beside me, always happy to be out of our 'stuffy apartment'.

I knelt down to pick up an odd leaf, this time genuinely taken by it. "Hmm."

Polimony broke her eyes from a bit of scenery, her tone dipped in sarcasm, *What's wrong? Is it too dry?*

I rotated the leaf; the side facing up was the ordinary cracked brown. The other side was an icy blue. I had noticed the unusual color on the edges of the leaf while walking toward it.

"No, it's just a blue leaf."

Polimony crinkled her nose at me. *You can't be too surprised that someone painted a leaf when you're planning on doing something similar.*

I shook my head in dismissal, "No, no. It isn't paint, it's as though it fell out this way."

You clearly put way too much gin in your coffee this morning. Maybe you should eat something.

The leaf crinkled as it found it's way into my pocket among the rest.

"I'm not saying you're right, but I could use something. This heartburn is suddenly killing me."

My legs began to shake as I stood up and reached for my flask. The initial burn soon subsided in favor of a soft warmth that radiated from my stomach. I don't think anyone really gets used to the cold.

Polimony shook her head as I tightened the lid, putting it back in my jacket.

You're hopeless. There's a café across the street. A muffin shouldn't cost much, and water is always free.

"You know, that isn't true. Some places charge you for the cup."

My muse cringed in response.

That should be criminal.

I shrugged weakly before another hint of blue flashed from a block away. I stopped and double took, was it that time already? A sparkling blue skirt across the street. There was a soft giggle from my right,

Her again? Gawk some more. It's only weird if you get caught, right?

I didn't have to look at a clock to know.

"Five thirty pm. Every day."

Every day by five twenty-nine pm, I would forget about that blue skirt. Every day at five thirty pm, I would be reminded of it. The longing stung; it stirred something beneath everything else. Each time I would hold onto it for a while, that way I could feel something genuine on a regular basis. The only drawback was that it also gave Polimony something to nag me about on a regular basis. I wasn't sure if it was worth it or not yet.

I don't know why you do this every. single. time. Just talk to her already. Or is it weird to talk to someone you've been staring at for the past several minutes?

"Several minutes!? And what does it matter, it's a high-risk situation."

She'd probably like you anyways. Especially if she's even half as weird as she looks. What do you risk losing for getting what you want?

"I don't want to lose the situation."

You are beyond dramatic. You're losing it every day by passively whining. Why not lost it actively instead?

I mulled that one over for a moment, then a brown maple leaf grabbed my attention from below. An absolutely vibrant sepia shade. I looked up as a set of heavy brakes sounded. She must have crossed over because now all I caught were blue streaks darting between the sea of legs in front of me. Was she moving? Or was that the crowd? A loud engine started up further away and faded. A bus must have just dropped off another wave of workers. Maple leaf again, a reddish brown this time. She was closer now. It was definitely *her* moving, but not as fast as the crowd. She kept stopping; repeatedly. A thin pale figure in black leggings, a patterned heart sweater, and her signature blue skirt. All topped off by sunny blonde hair. From this far I could've mistook her for Anna. A memory of my ex began playing itself on repeat in my head. I tried to shake away the flashback, choosing to instead focus on Blue Skirt's outfit. It was the teasing caricature of femininity that kept me in the now, and right now I needed to break routine. I swam through the crowd towards her, closing the gap between us.

Polimony followed suit, keeping up behind me. *Do you wonder if maybe you're the tease, and really it's her that is creeping on you?*

Polimony's input was unwelcome, the sarcastic tone even more so. Maybe I needed to spite her. Maybe I had something to prove to myself. Maybe I was already sick of looking at leaves and wanted to look at something else for a little while. This time, when that sparkling blue skirt was within view again, I spoke up. "Hey, uh - Howdy."

Oh. My. God.

My greeting hobbled out of me and bounced off of her. She continued walking, oblivious to my verbal foible.

At least she didn't hear that.

I made haste, speed walking at a pace just beneath that of a street predator.

On the prowl, are we?

"Shut up!"

I choked. Out loud. Nobody noticed and I kept on. Finally, she was within literal reach, so I tapped her on the shoulder. This was the closest to her that I had ever been. Bright blue flashed by as she spun around to face me, a stack of pamphlets in her hands.

A set of inquisitive brown eyes looked me over. "What?"

"Well..."

"Well... what?"

Blue Skirt innocently smiled despite how painfully awkward I felt.

Ask for a pamphlet you moron. Look how tall that stack is.

Tall? It took me a moment to figure out what Polimony was getting at.

"Well, I'd like a pamphlet, and I'd like you to tell me what the pamphlet is all about!"

Now you have a moment to remember basic conversational skills.

The expression on Blue Skirt's face brightened. "Wonderful! It's actually a very welcoming club, and the fact that you were so excited to touch me is proof that you are ready to join!"

I relaxed, smiling. This sounded like my kind of club.

Blue Skirt handed me a pamphlet and continued, "I knew you would tap me anyways. That's actually what this is all about, we meet on Sundays!"

... I waited for her to continue, but that was all. Her statement was finished.

Stowing away the pamphlet, I continued to politely wait for more information. There was nothing. She just stared at me with a huge smile across her face.

I cleared my throat slightly. "When on Sundays? And also, where, and who?"

My confused tone didn't register with her at all, "It is all in the pamphlet. When you read it, you will understand."

I tried to conceal a pout. Her voice was soft at least. It soothed what was now starting to come off as a creative rejection. Though, I wasn't sure if I had yet made a solicitation for her to reject. She spun around and dazzled me again before I could get more information, weaving between pockets of people and eventually evading my sight.

I felt Polimony's head rest against my shoulder as Blue Skirt's afterimage faded behind her. *You could've definitely done worse. I think.*

I inspected the pamphlet. Simple white copy paper, printed with the title 'Clairvoyant Sundays'. The subtitle advertised 'a meeting for clairvoyant individuals interested in collaborating.' The inside was completely blank, as was the back. I suppose the truly gifted among us would know when and where to meet.

Pretty and crazy. Exactly your type Simon, don't you think?

Leaves crinkled as I crammed the pamphlet back in my pocket.

I gave Polimony a smirk, "I'm definitely lured in by a certain amount of eccentricity. The skirt helps too."

Polimony brushed my arm and looked down at the sidewalk.

So... that muffin and water?

Right as she said that I realized how lightheaded I had become over the course of my conversation with Blue Skirt. "Tony's?"

Not this time, we went there yesterday.

"Ah."

She didn't have to eat, and rarely did. And yet two days in a row was still too much Tony's for her.

"Cheap corner stand it is."

There was always tomorrow.

A meek demeanor and a few dollars is what it takes to get a cup of water and a muffin. Some days it felt like everything was getting more expensive. On those same days it could also feel like everything was getting so cheap. I took heaping bites of a stale muffin, washing it down with water and the occasional sneaky sip of the flask. The sun was beginning its descent, and the breeze was becoming still. Crisp, decaying, plant matter continued to crunch with each step. More and more cracks were visible in the sidewalk below as we made our way in the direction of the third ward. At this point we were walking for the fun of it. My pocket crinkled with every other step. There were enough leaves to make me feel like I'd accomplished something for the day. I was sloppily wiping crumbs and stray liquor from my lower lip when I saw a flash of blue in my peripheral vision. I whipped around just in time to see her round the corner of an older brick and mortar barber shop. She was one street over. I hooked a left and then a right. Now she was just a block away.

I guess now that she's spoken to you anything goes. Go get 'em tiger.

"I'm in the zone, and I'm not that type of person."

A person who literally chases women?

"It isn't a chase, I just want to know where her base of operations is, so to speak."

Probably her home, where she feels safe and secure.

I almost stopped, suddenly aware of how odd the things I was saying aloud were. Luckily, I am often reminded how little attention is paid by people in public. At least, that is usually the case in a city as dense as ours. I continued to observe Blue Skirt from afar, making sure to keep a cautious distance. The awkward feeling that accompanied stalking someone went away as I grew more engrossed with each observation. I wanted to see where else she went, what else she did, maybe it would explain the pamphlet. Or maybe it would keep me occupied for a while. In any case, she kept on. Bobbing from street to street, across concrete and asphalt. Finally she came upon an unattended purse resting on a bench at a bus stop. She opened it and paused for a moment, then crammed a pamphlet inside. It was fascinating to witness the rest of her routine, watching her squirrel away pamphlets in seemingly random places. Pamphlets made their way into random mailboxes, under windshield wipers, various nooks and crannies, each less sensible than the last. I couldn't make out a method to her madness. She spent a fair bit of time doing this, the sun slowly setting with each stop. Street by street I persisted in my pursuit, occasionally having to hide myself from the odd glance here and there. Eventually, the gentle hug of clean buildings and high rises was replaced by the vice-like grip of broken windows and slumped red brick. The grim structures loomed over cracked streets, every other block unlit. The walk dragged on until finally Blue Skirt reached a decaying cinder block tower. Green particle board and old ac units filled most of the window spaces on its face. The few lights that illuminated the exterior did little to mask the intimidating ominousness of the structure. I watched as Blue Skirt walked up the steps, and into the concrete dungeon. Above the entrance, faded print read: 'St. Ivy Houses.'

Are you satisfied?

I flinched, startled by Polimony's voice after an hour or so of silent stalking.

"To be honest? Absolutely not. I have no idea what to do now."

However, I did note the address to myself out loud so I wouldn't forget. "6000 South 46th Street". Polimony giggled as I whispered the address to myself repeatedly.

Oh no no no. You're a complete creep now. If there was any doubt before...

"No... no... I just like to remember things."

Selectively remembering things that only a creep would. Like an oblivious woman's address.

I'd had enough of her sarcasm. "You really ought to mind your own business!"

YOU dragged me out here! Your business IS my business!

Two stories above, a light turned on and a window opened. indication enough that it was time to leave. I sucked in a breath and walked away. I knew part of her route, and now I knew where it ended. I had found my next work of art. That was enough for today.

II

6000 South 46th Street. The address would continue to circulate my dreams all throughout the night.

6000 South 46th Street. The address alone was almost enough to wake me.

...

BEEP! BEEP! BEEP!

My eyes were already open. For the first time in months, I was awake before Polimony. I excitedly silenced our bedside alarm, beaming with satisfaction. Today I was a productive person. I needed a machine to wake me up. My mind had things to do that my body was not ready for; things that were urgent and simply couldn't wait until I woke up naturally. Polimony rolled over, still half asleep.

Why. Are. You. Awake.

I relished the exhausted rasp in her voice, "I have business. Me! And by extension, you!"

I know I called you lazy and unemployed. This isn't what I wanted.

For just a while, I'd let her think she could roll back over.

I shouldn't have made such a big deal about waking up late. I'm sorry.

I let her apology sink in, I felt so smug. She hardly ever did that. This was too good to be true.

Just go back to bed, let's just go back to sleep.

I listened as she got comfortable again, taking my silence as some sort of implicit agreement. Then I shot out from under the covers and raced to her side of the bed. "BEEP, BEEP, BEEP!"

The skin by her eyes creased as she strained to keep them shut. "BEEP, BEEP, BEEP!"

This must have been how she felt every morning. "BEEP, BEEP, BEEP!"

She rolled out of bed and onto the floor before I had a chance to start shaking her.

"What happened? Did you fall?"

I get it, I get it, please just let me get dressed and we'll do whatever you want.

"Whatever I want?"

I'm getting dressed.

Polimony shuffled to the closet. I rushed to the kitchen and opened the fridge. I was so excited already, and for some reason I felt the need to keep all my wits about me. That meant today was a soda day, another 'first time in months'. I reached to the back of the bottom shelf, palming a lukewarm Eleven Up or whatever.

I popped the tab and gingerly sipped it, absentmindedly beginning to think aloud to my muse. "You know, most of these soda recipes haven't even been around for more than a couple human life spans."

She groggily slumped into the kitchen and sat at the table. *Your point being?*

I allowed another wave of bubbles to sink down my throat before continuing. "My point being that we don't know what this does if you drink it every day for one hundred years."

Thank God no one ever lives that long... Especially you Simon.

I raised an eyebrow at her.

Cirrhosis.

A sick grin formed on her face as she let her head sink to the table.

I crinkled my now empty soda can and threw it in the trash with a frown. "I would quit drinking if only to make you suffer with me a little longer."

I cut my eyes from the trash back to her, narrowing them on the way.

"And even if I don't, twenty more years can be made to feel like a hundred. Even for you."

Polimony momentarily raised her head, shooting me a dismissive look of contempt. *A hundred years is an arbitrary number on a long enough timespan. You don't even know what a hundred years means, and you haven't lived long enough to forget.*

I opened my mouth to laugh but nothing came out. The statement was sickeningly true. I felt an intense itch, deep inside my stomach, as a handful of memories played in my head. My ex-girlfriend Anna used to ponder these things with me. When she used to be fun, that short while before fun became a problem to her. When she was willing to admit just how much we had in common. Before she began to see me as something broken and unlovable. I remembered what it felt like to be loved in spite of myself...

Hello?

Polimony appeared suddenly alert and concerned. I physically shook away the memory, forcing myself to return to the present. "I'm fine, just zoned out for a moment."

Polimony's expression remained. *Okay... Well, where in the world did you put all that stuff from yesterday?*

"Oh!"

I ran to the bedroom. I didn't even need to open the hamper. It was already so full the lid was stuck open. My jacket was resting on top of an intimidatingly tall pile of dirty clothes, the pockets waiting to be looked through. I fished through them and returned to the kitchen, dumping the contents onto the kitchen table in front of my muse.

"I must have been really excited last night, I almost washed all of this!"

Polimony shook her head at me. *You ruined your leaves.*

It was true, they were all crinkled and torn. It didn't really matter though. "I was going to shred them all anyway."

My eyes lazily drifted towards the crumpled-up pamphlet. The excitement of the morning had already begun to wear off as the day worked its way into me. "I still don't know what to make of yesterday."

Polimony blinked in disbelief. *What?*

"I said I don't know what to make of yesterday."

I heard you. Simon, you followed a woman to her home then ran away in the dead of night. What do you mean you don't know what to make of yesterday? Why did you wake me up if you didn't have a plan for today?

"Hmm. To be honest, I was just excited that an alarm woke me up instead of you. I actually don't remember the original reason I set it. But there was certainly a reason, and that excites me! Do you recall anything from last night? Because, well... I don't..."

Polimony stared at me blankly.

I smoothed out the balled-up pamphlet on the table, trying to remember. "I think I was feeling a bit shaken by myself, and I couldn't sleep. I might have had a quick nightcap or two..."

Okay, you know what, I'm going back to bed.

I read the front. 'Clairvoyant Sundays', "Wait, what day is it today?"

Polimony paused in the doorway to the bedroom and appeared to literally seethe with frustration. *I don't know Simon. What day was it yesterday?*

"It was... The bus. Everyone was out at four. But they didn't look as dead inside as usual... Probably Friday?"

So you have a day to figure that crap out. Goodnight. Or good morning. Somehow I feel like you've taken both from me.

I rushed after her into the bedroom, but she was gone.

"Whatever, I can investigate these things without you anyways. It's only," dim red numbers advertised the time from across the room, "five thirty?" I looked around and listened. Still nothing. I wish I could just disappear when *she* pissed *me* off.

A few minutes had to pass before I could trust that Polimony wasn't just lurking about silently. I let out a defeated sigh. My feet auto-piloted me to the liquor cabinet. "Gin, gin, get it in. Coffee, coffee..."

A cursory glance at the half open can of coffee grounds revealed it to be empty. "Hmm."

I needed an excuse to go outside this early anyway. The streets would be comfortably empty. "Gin, gin, still get in..." I sang, filling my flask and donning a loose-fitting sweater. Before I left, I paused one last time and listened for that unfamiliar silence. It was only me.

The clop of hardwood was exchanged for the familiar tap of concrete as I walked out of the apartment building. Brisk early-morning air bit at my exposed neck. I had underestimated how cold it would be, but a walk up the stairs wasn't worth a proper jacket. At one end of the street the sun teased the horizon, a narrow slit of pink wedged between concrete. Opposite the urban sunrise was the decaying image of night; The last hints of darkness sinking beneath black asphalt. I wanted to get a cup of coffee before the sun woke everyone else up, and there was only one place nearby that was open this early.

Lorretta's had occupied the corner of 23rd and Main for a few years now. It was a retro themed diner that, despite its hearty attempt, had failed to pique the interest of more than a niche crowd of regulars. I liked it though, its lack of success attracted people like me who gravitated towards the more vacant. I passed by the side windows of the diner and froze. A flash of blue had struck my peripheral vision through the glass. I had to double take before I turned in a panic, drowning myself in half a flasks worth of gin. A different top and a similar skirt. It had to have been her, she had a unique style with a signature lower half. I couldn't imagine another human being that would completely bedazzle a pleat skirt in blue. I didn't have the pamphlet, and when I thought about it, I didn't see any with her. Maybe this was her off time. I let a wave of inebriation wash over me before I walked past the windows again. Breathing a sigh of relief, I opened the painted glass door to the inner dining area. None of the staff were present, she was the only person inside. Her head turned towards me and tilted slightly.

Straight brown hair framed her face and barely teased her left shoulder with the movement. I took my hands out of my pockets then put them back, nervous to be in her sight.

She smiled and took care of the awkwardness for both of us. "Hey, what're you doing over there?"

She gestured towards the empty stool beside her. I slowly walked over but had to stop as she suddenly stood up and shook her head. "Wait, I'm being weird, let's just sit at a booth," her smile faltered slightly, "I don't think that the only two people eating in a restaurant should eat separately."

I must have looked as puzzled as I felt to provoke such an explanation.

The red faux leather of the booth was just as slippery as the stools. It was a struggle to not perpetually slide down towards a grimy checker-tiled abyss. I finally found a sweet spot as a worn cook burst from the bathroom at the other end of the diner. "Sorry, sorry," he apologized hurriedly, drying his hands on his apron, "we've been short staffed lately."

It was nice that he washed his hands, but I knew the apron was dirty. Definitely just getting coffee. A heavyset waitress suddenly crept out of the same bathroom as the cook. She eyed us both before slinking into the kitchen. The cook readjusted his apron a few times and followed her.

Blue Skirt giggled. "I love drama. The same things seem to happen everywhere, don't they?"

I struggled to swallow nothing and took my hands out of my pockets. "Yes, I suppose so."

My eyes dragged back and forth between the shiny table and hers. The quiet was shredding me to bits but she seemed completely unfazed by it, amused almost. The waitress finally came back holding a yellow notepad and a silver pen; she clicked it a dozen or so times on the way over. Her sneaky and meek demeanor had been replaced by, what I assumed was, her usual passive aggressive one. She looked up from her notepad at me, confused. "Have I served you sir?"

I shook my head no.

"Well, what would you like to drink tonight," She corrected herself, "today?"

"A coffee," I eyed the bathroom, recalling what I had just seen. "Just a coffee. Not too hot."

The waitress put her notepad in her pocket without writing anything. "Not too hot?"

"Yes, I want to be able to drink it right away."

"Hot's the only temperature it comes in."

I stared at her, annoyed.

You could almost see the cogs turning in her head as she released a quiet groan. "I'll see what I can do."

She dragged herself back into the kitchen, the swivel door dramatically swinging open and shut behind her. There was a sudden commotion and yelling in the kitchen then she was out again, holding a coffee pot, a mug, and a small cup of ice cubes. All three were placed on the table in a single swift motion. Before I knew it she was gone again, leaving Blue Skirt and I alone. I had no idea how to broach the subject of the pamphlet. My first instinct was to bullshit her, but a part of me was worried she might actually be clairvoyant. No, that's nonsense. Right? She sipped at her coffee and maintained eye contact with me. I hadn't noticed before, but she had perfectly green eyes.

You know, it's not that crazy.

No, not right now, go away Polimony!

Blue Skirt giggled, *My name's actually Rachel. I figured you would know that... You're usually really good at prying.*

Prying?

Yeah, yesterday? And before?

I filled my mug with coffee, unable to do anything else.

Rachel shot me a confused look followed by a blank stare. "But, you can hear me?"

My hands trembled as I brought the mug to my lips, scalding myself with the first sip. "AH!"

In a confused state of shock, I had forgotten to put any ice in it.

She chuckled at me and pulled a blue pen from somewhere inside of her sweater. "I didn't think this was how this would go, but I love poetry anyways."

She swiped a napkin from the edge of the table and began to furiously scribble on it. I watched as she filled the white square with cute blue lettering. Finally, she crumpled it up and threw it at me.

"This should help," she paused for a moment, suddenly hesitant. "The gifted among us can decipher this. I have to go."

I got one last good look into those vibrant green eyes before a less vibrant dull dollar was planted on the table. Then, she was gone. I made sure she wasn't by the windows and opened up the napkin. Its rough surface contrasted nicely with the table's glossy finish.

A secret between two left alone here,
abandoned to none it seemed clear,
a home to those forgotten and small,
though the building itself stands tall,
surrounded by many its history old,
eight seven eight one a number is told,
when the time is right the sun will set,
the secrets will sleep soundly in bed,
on the day of God a clock will sound,
that's when all meetings ought to bound.
- R :)

I smoothed out the napkin once more and folded it up, exchanging it in my pocket for the flask. The rest of its contents quickly made its way into my coffee, along with a few ice cubes.

III

As a portrait painter, I spend a lot of time drawing caricatures. Not the kind you buy on a pier, under a hot sun, for an often temporary partner. I draw the kind where the exaggeration is more subtle, the kind meant to deceive rather than amuse. It isn't enough to be beautiful. It isn't even enough to be adorable. I embellish the present, preserving only the best observations for the future.

I've painted every woman that I've dated in the past several years. Often, the finished pieces were sold through Marcus on consignment. He actually inspired the emotionally motivated side hustle, but over time it became a neurotic habit. I like painting portraits; I like to dream. The only downside is that I dream just as much when I paint my partners. Each embellishment made out of habit brings to mind the idiosyncrasies left out. In the end, I'm left with someone who doesn't exist: A dream that I love more than the original subject.

But it is just like any art. You should obsess over and chase a dream, struggle to capture it even. But you shouldn't fall in love with one.

...

The plaster ceiling above our bed became a vacuous white void if you stared at it long enough. It sucked away all thought with its vast emptiness.

I had been staring at it, thinking about Rachel's poem, for the better part of an hour. "Day of God, that confirms that we meet on Sundays. Right?"

Polimony faced away from me, her gaze cast out our bedroom window at the street below.

Why are you so stuck on that? The front of her pamphlet says, 'Clairvoyant Sundays' on it.

I frowned, still staring at the ceiling. "What if it's a red herring and she's actually Jewish?"

Polimony ignored me. *If people are ants from a plane, what are they from here? Cattle? They look bigger than ants right now.*

"There's no way they look as big as cattle, we're three stories up. I thought you said you'd help me with this."

I said I'd be your sounding board.

"Sounding boards don't talk."

Now you're being rude. It's on Sunday, you knew that an hour ago. You knew that yesterday. You're absolutely terrible at this when you drink.

"I just don't want to get anything wrong."

Polimony rerouted her attention back to the people below, *If they aren't cows, are they a smaller animal or a bigger bug?*

I ignored her, mentally labeling Sunday as a fact so that I could move on. "At least the clock is an obvious gimme."

There was only one cliché clock tower in the entire city: the T.M. Warren Clock in the middle of the Third Ward. "The Warren Tower only chimes twice a day now, midnight and noon."

Polimony turned around, apparently satisfied with my sudden progress. *'The sun will set', probably midnight.*

"And we know it'll be within earshot of the chime. That isn't too big of an area. Especially when you consider buildings blocking the sound.

It just said a clock will sound. It never mentioned it being heard.

I forced the extra uncertainty from my mind before it could stump me again. I really was useless when I drank.

"Sunday at midnight for sure. At least there's that."

I stretched out further and relaxed a bit, satisfied with determining a fact.

Polimony turned around and stared at me. She had that look on her face again, the one she makes when I say something she thinks is stupid.

I frowned in return, always unsure of what provoked it. "What?"

I don't know why you look so pleased. That's in less than sixteen hours.

I sat up straight and mulled that over for a second before my heart sank a little. She was right. Midnight on Sunday is the start of Sunday, not the end. I had to be somewhere still unknown, practically tonight. My stomach growled quietly. I needed another drink, but I didn't want to feel it crawl up my throat for the next couple of hours. In any case, I needed to eat something. Polimony must have heard my stomach, she had already rushed off to the closet and began the usual racket.

"I haven't even thought about a place to eat at yet... Was my stomach really that loud?"

The impossibly loud clatter of hangers stopped momentarily.

Yes, it was, and it's fine because I'm picking this time.

"How is that fair? *I'm* the one who has to actually eat the food."

And yet somehow you always make the wrong choice. This time I choose...

She slowly emerged from the closet with her fingers pressed against her head, putting on a dramatic show of deep thought, *Loretta's.*

"Ha, ha. Incredible. It's incredible that you are so funny. Absolutely not."

Polimony chuckled softly, *Why's that funny?*

I hadn't told her about seeing Rachel, something about what she'd said had jarred me into secrecy.

"Screw it, let's just figure it out as we go. I don't want anything here and I think we need a distraction for a bit."

Once again I was out and about, this time joined by Polimony. The sky had become dark and overcast, sending most of the usual Saturday city-goers indoors in anticipation of cold rainfall. The empty streets and low light made for a very cozy midday stroll. I inhaled deeply, savoring the cold muggy air. The touch of humidity had actually softened it to my taste. Cafés and restaurants dotted the sides of Main Street but today none of them seemed appealing. The next numbered street came into view on the right. Northeast 23rd. I stopped mid-stride as I recalled what Northeast 23rd was home too. "I think I fancy myself a bagel! I know where we're eating now."

Polimony kept walking, ignoring my dramatic stop, and sighed as she passed me. *Somehow, always the wrong choice.*

Tony's Illegal Bakery was arguably the most interesting bakery in the city. It was certainly the most interesting bakery off of Northeast 23rd. The bakery itself was presumably legal. Being only a couple blocks off Main Street, and a few more from a police station, it would be very impressive if it were as illegal as Tony claimed. Fake metal rivets framed the pompous barred doors of the bakery's entrance. The building itself was a replica of a metal barracks, the kind straight out of an old twentieth century war film. A few tables inside were occupied by seemingly ordinary individuals. Though, given the name of the establishment, it was more fun to assume that they were engaged in only the most devious of activities. I darted past, towards the front counter, marveling at the pastry lined shelves on display. An absolute monster of a lad was waiting at the register. He was dressed in an ill-fitting pink and light blue tuxedo, grinning ear to ear. He towered over Polimony and I.

Despite his lumbering appearance, his voice was devoid of any bass, "Welcome to our bakery brother, what can I get you today?"

I didn't look at the pastries for long, I knew what I was there for. "I want an illegal bagel, with some of Tony's... secret cheese."

The lad struggled to hold back his laughter, "That'll be two seventy-five. Would you like some coffee with that, brother?"

"Yes actually, can I get a double shot with some... creepy cream?"

He was beginning to visibly strain. "F-four twenty-five then... *big man...*"

Tears started streaming down his face as he tried to finish his sentence, "I'll have that... We'll have that right out for you."

He yelled out my order of secret cheese and creepy cream before hunching over, his hand on his abdomen. He sucked in a smile, and I could see a couple veins forming on his head.

I gave him a minute to recover before asking where Tony was.

"Uh... Oh, yeah he's in the back... Sorry I just started."

Sweat trickled down the now bulging veins in the tortured man's forehead. I nodded in acknowledgment. Polimony snickered.

Better make sure none of Tony's secret cheese makes it into your creepy cream coffee.

I chuckled in acknowledgment of her crude joke. This was a fun place, and a very effective distraction from the puzzle that was weighing on me. I looked down, even the floor was impossible to take seriously. Every purple tile had a different cartoon pastry crudely drawn on it. They looked like someone had done them with permanent marker. I waited patiently at the counter. Eventually, another gigantic man sneakily handed off a brown paper bag to our cashier. He crept off before quickly returning with a lidded paper cup. The cashier looked at me, still trying hard to maintain a serious expression.

I slipped him a five-dollar bill. "Keep the change"

He started to look like he was in pain, pushing 'the goods' across the counter towards me. "Don't tell anyone where you got this"

Somehow this backwards method of advertisement had managed to keep Tony's Illegal Bakery drowning in business.

I faked a secretive whisper, "I was never here!"

He finally doubled over in an all-consuming fit of hysterical laughter. Polimony and I casually walked towards the front doors. It was not uncommon for new employees to behave this way.

As I pushed open the left side, a coarse voice shouted something from behind us. "I don't care how new you are! I told you the rule! YOU'RE FIRED!"

I turned around in surprise, that was Tony! The now ex-cashier kept laughing. He appeared to be underneath the counter with a handful of co-workers staring down at him. Despite the hysteria of the man's laughter, they all wore somber expressions as Tony continued to berate him for breaking character.

The clouds still loomed above us outside. Somehow, in the ten odd minutes it took to get a bagel from Tony's, the temperature had dropped even further. The wind had picked up as well, whipping through my coat. I held the paper bag against me like it was an infant breastfeeding. I didn't want it to get cold, and it was still too hot for me to eat anyway. I began to picture myself as a rather mannish woman, breastfeeding a baby with a bagel for a head. It was enough to make me laugh out loud. I always imagined I'd be a single parent, raising whatever unfortunate child I'd brought from a divorce. I imagined raising them alongside Polimony. Somehow, someway, that could work. Polimony leaned against me as we walked back towards Main Street. If anyone could see her, they'd probably mistake us for a couple. I allowed the fantasy to run through my head, stirring up a line from the cryptic poem Rachel had given me. 'A certain secret between two'.

Finally, it clicked. "A certain secret between two!"

Polimony took her weight off me and gave me a look, *The poem?*

"A home to those forgotten and small..."

I thought we went out to think of something else for a while. You have the rest of-

I shook my head at her, I needed to think aloud, "A secret, forgotten and small. The kind shared by two. A secret that has no home until it finds a home. A kid Polimony, an orphan! An orphanage!"

Polimony stared at the sidewalk for a moment, a touch of sadness in her voice when she spoke, *There's one, for better or for worse. It's by the Warren Tower in the Third Ward too. It's within earshot of the chime. Maybe your theory wasn't that far-fetched.*

That, or Rachel hurriedly wrote this on a napkin and didn't have time to be more subtle.

"Time. Place. Everything else we can play by ear."

Polimony put on a weak smile. She didn't like it when I was away from her and that included mentally. Unfortunately, as the poem began to drift from my mind it was replaced by the subject of my next portrait. Admittedly, I had wanted to do something with leaves and plants around the city for a while. What I lacked was a subject I was passionate about. Now I had one: Rachel. The piece was already beginning to materialize in my mind, but I needed more face time with her to flesh out the specifics. For all intents and purposes, I had a date with her tonight. But until then one detail was obviously going to make it's way into the work: a brilliant blue to dominate the lower half. The kind of brilliance I wanted wasn't going to be found at a traditional store. There was one person I had for these kinds of things. A lump formed in my stomach. It was the same person I'd been avoiding for the past few months.

IV

I had met Marcus, coincidentally, through an ex. Amber or Amanda, it was hard to recall. She never introduced me to him, and she denied knowing him. He bumped into me at an event and claimed that she was an absolute freak. We talked for a while about the weird things she was into, for better or for worse. Even if he didn't actually know her, he definitely knew enough about her. I believed him, and it was enough to trust him when he gave me his card and claimed to have the 'best supplies that any artist needs.'

That was several years and several months ago.

...

The city bus rounded a corner onto 4th Avenue. It had been a calm ride into the fancy First Ward. Very unlike the usual uncomfortable chaos that was the 'Mass Transit Experience.' Eventually the bus lurched to a stop in front of a bright blue bench. There wasn't the usual awning, but that was okay. It hadn't yet begun to rain. The heavy monochromatic sky did nothing to dull the colorful buildings that lined 4th Avenue. Every shop seemed to have its own theme, each dominated by a different shade of what have you. Locals affectionately called this strip of visual variety 'Rainbow Street'. Not only for the colors, but because each pastel point of sale advertised crafty things. Only one of them was on the agenda though. I had no interest in securing our apartment or buying binoculars to spy on my opposite-sex neighbors; That could wait for another day. No, my destination was about two blocks down. Another brightly painted, stucco covered, concrete cube. This one was colored a groovy green and was my old friend Marcus' main place of business. The actual structure of the paint shop was beginning to show its age, the branching cracks in the stucco dated it like the rings of a tree. Three short steps led to a solid oak door, subtly barring anyone who used a wheelchair from entering. A bell rang as we walked into the comfortably petite interior. Rows of shelves lined the walls with merchandise stacked to the ceiling. The stocky and vaguely foreign man that I had come to know as Mark stood behind the register. He was facing away from us, intently arranging some tubes of paint along the wall.

The shop bell rang again as the door slowly shut, this time catching his attention. "Prices are based on shelf level, see me for top shelf items – " his eyes lit up as they met mine. "Ah yes, Toby isn't it?"

In all fairness, Marcus knew faces better than he knew names. However by this point he absolutely knew mine.

I wasn't going to give him the pleasure of purposely goofing my name, only for me to get his correct. "No Mike, it's Simon."

I grinned playfully as Polimony wandered around the shop.

Simon, it's a pity that a clever man such as yourself has considered shop lifting. These shelves have plenty of nice tubes of blue stuff, let's put that five-finger discount to good use!

I ignored her terrible idea. A brief flash of annoyance must have made its way across my face.

Marcus pouted. "Touché *Simon*, and don't look so grouchy. It is only a game between two friends, but how long has it been since I've seen my favorite customer and painter! Are you really getting back to work?" His eyes darted to the door as he dropped to a whisper, "Are you here for the usual?"

I shook my head before he could duck below the counter. "No, no, that's fine, Mark. I came here for one thing and one thing only. I need something to make blue paint with, I've met this girl and –"

He put a finger up and hit a switch under the counter, locking the entrance remotely. "Buddy, you came into my shop asking for materials to paint a fine bitc– I mean fine *woman?* I will only give you the best. Nothing on these shelves will do! Please join me downstairs."

With that, he disappeared beneath the counter. This was a painfully obvious up-sell, but what he lacked in fair pricing was always made up for in quality. I quickly locked the front door and flipped the 'open' sign to 'closed.' Then I followed him behind the counter. Two floorboards formed the hidden trap door to Marcus' basement. Besides how new they appeared relative to the boards around them, they hardly gave away their true purpose. The entrance had to be hidden because the basement was not part of the original building plans. Even if they were, the deviation still wasn't up to city code. A lack of a ramp was one thing, an illegal basement was another. For this reason, Marcus only invited VIPs to his hidden lair. As far as I was aware, that list was rather short and did not include any members of code enforcement. Polimony was staring at some brushes against a back wall when I gestured for her to follow me 'downstairs'.

She feigned extreme excitement, *Well of course I will follow you into Marcus' basement! Only the best things happen down there!*

I frowned. She had no reason to be so sarcastic, I had already denied 'the usual.'

Each step creaked on the way down, only adding to the creepy dungeon aesthetic. This would make sense, if the horrible condition of the stares didn't so deeply contrast with the rest of the 'basement.' Calling his underground room a 'basement' was actually doing an extreme disservice. It was deceptively spacious given the square footage of the shop above. The walls were done in a red brick façade and the support beams were dark stained cedar. A grid of riveted metal drawers occupied the wall to the right, the design reminiscent of a morgue. How they were organized, only Marcus knew; but his collection was expansive. A rectangular glass dining set was situated to the left, a steel scale in the center. Since I had last visited, he had redone the lighting with various tinted lights and hung up a handful of modern abstract pieces. Marcus was already shoulder deep in one of the large drawers. Polimony walked behind him, appearing to peak inside.

I shot a look at her. Our eyes met and she frowned.

I'm not a ghost Simon. I can't see anything you can't.

I nodded my head silently, and she resumed her useless peaking. Sometimes it was easy to forget the limitations of our situation, especially when she acted as though it was something supernatural. He continued to rummage about in the deep drawer, releasing a bothersome array of sounds in the process. I couldn't help but cringe. The sounds hinted towards the contents being composed of a diversity of materials. But it wasn't the sounds that bothered me. The rummaging simply felt inappropriate. It implied that what he was searching for was loosely buried among an assortment of random things, all of which were valuable enough to warrant the need for special storage. The entire arrangement seemed self-contradictory. Before I could think about it any further, he fished out a wooden box that appeared unscathed by the racket. He gently shut the drawer and placed it on the table, taking a seat in front of it. I sat across from him, pulling an empty chair out beside me for Polimony.

Marcus didn't notice, he was too engrossed in dramatically opening the box. "My friend, you will see this was worth the wait. You wanted blue? You wanted special? Behold."

Marcus slowly pulled a silk bag from the box, undoing the string to reveal a fist sized pile of ultra-fine semitransparent blue gems.

"Mark, what am I looking at here?"

A wide toothy smile broke out across Marcus' face. "Pulverized, jeweler grade, blue diamonds!"

Polimony's mouth dropped, *I was wrong, please buy coke instead.*

Marcus must have seen the look on *my* face because he quickly put his hands up and explained, "I know, I know, I haven't seen you for a while; I am sure this is another one of those 'bad times' for you. But my friend, please don't worry about it. Do you know how many times I've ripped you off?"

I opened my mouth to say something, but he didn't let me speak, "Rhetorical question. The point is, I didn't pay for these. It was more of an 'off the books' acquisition. You'd be doing me a favor by taking some off my hands."

Polimony sank further into her chair, apparently dazed, *Of course! Every time you drag me down here! Only the best things happen!*

My hands shook as I ignored Polimony and reached for my flask, emptying the contents into my stomach with a single dramatic pull. "Mark... Mark this is so far beyond what I expected."

He proudly nodded his head. "I know! I told you: I will only give you the best! Also, I think you will love the price that I am about to offer them for."

I shook my head, struggling to overcome my own shock. "No, Mark, this is too much. You're right, this is a bad time for me. And no! Before you offer, I don't want any kind of front. Especially not for fucking diamonds. You said you didn't pay for them?"

He put up a hand to silence me. "Too many questions, friend. No fronts. Only cash. But! - I will certainly pass my savings on to you in the form of a fair price."

He pressed a couple buttons on the scale, zeroing it, then poured a small pile of the diamonds onto the shiny surface. I stayed quiet as it loaded. 40.001 grams. Incredibly accurate. Marcus beamed at his own eyeballing abilities. "You know what, I'll even round it down and price it for forty grams exactly. Just for you, old friend!"

He reached out to shake my hand but I didn't meet him, instead I kept my eyes fixated on the pile of literal diamonds on the table.

He cleared his throat. "Ten thousand. Even."

I reached my hand halfway to his. "Five thousand. You paid nothing for these."

He hesitated slightly, bringing his hand a mere inch from mine. "Eight thousand. Firm. I am being nice buddy, these are jeweler grade. You are paying 'pennies on the dollar.' If even that much."

"Why would someone crush something like this? How would they crush something like this?"

"NO MORE QUESTIONS!"

I had to concede, finally giving him a proper handshake. My stomach turned as the diamonds glittered.

"Simon, stop looking at them like that! You will not regret this my friend. The stones alone will make up for themselves with the value added to your piece."

The alcohol was doing little to delay the buyer's remorse, and I hadn't even paid yet.

"Can I write you a check?"

Marcus beamed.

"Absolutely my friend! But it better clear!"

I grabbed my chest, and then my checkbook. This needed to pay off. It really, really, needed to.

V

I can't even remember when I started *really* drinking. I know it wasn't that bad before Anna. I would have the nightly glass of gin but it was on the rocks, not a full glass. I began to take the ice out when she moved in, a few glasses during the day shortly after. When I try to recall what triggered it I draw a blank. It's different from a black out though; in that it isn't just an empty space where a memory is supposed to be. There's something there, but even when I manage to grab it I can't hold on for very long. It almost feels like the memory isn't mine anymore, as though I am trying to pull it from the hands of another. Maybe that's for the best.

There's no telling whether they are even worth remembering anyways.

...

It had finally begun to rain. I made the last pot of coffee for the night as Polimony read at the kitchen table. In front of her a small silk pouch, full of pulverized diamonds, sat unsuspectingly beside a few tubes of paint. She hadn't said anything the entire way from Marcus' shop. The front door was locked, and my heart was still racing from the bus ride and walk home. Something about carrying a bag of diamonds did that to you. Our coffee pot slowly filled with dark liquid. The kind that would keep you awake and alert in the middle of the night.

"I really hope she didn't mean midnight Monday; do you think she might've made a mistake?"

Polimony shrugged and continued to read her book, her face as expressionless as marble.

I rapped my fingers on the counter top as the coffee maker continued to bubble. "I mean, it's kind of an infamous time to set, right? Midnight? Very ambiguous."

Polimony flipped a page, ignoring me.

"Hello? I'm nervous as hell here. What are you reading anyway?"

I crept behind her, trying to get a peak. The pages were blank, of course. She had manifested a book for the sole purpose of ignoring me. Her head turned slightly backward, and then cocked back towards the empty pages. A minimal acknowledgment of my presence. Then she flipped a page, saying nothing still.

"Are you mad? Is it the diamonds?"

Her voice cut through the air between us, quiet yet full of pent-up anger,

Yes. I'm still mad that you spent half of our emergency fund on art supplies.

"*My* emergency fund. And don't say 'art supplies' all condescending like that. It's not like I dropped a grand on paint. They *are* diamonds. And we got a great deal on them!"

Polimony flipped a page again, silently disagreeing with me.

The coffee maker ran out of water to boil, and hissed for bit. With the completion of its task it chimed and clicked off, Leaving the entire room silent. I made a cup and refilled my flask with gin, making sure to check the time as well. Eleven o six blinked monochromatically on the coffee maker's LCD. The orphanage was twenty minutes away by monorail, far faster than a taxi at this time of night. I chugged my coffee and grabbed the diamonds, making a beeline for the bedroom. The silk bag slid effortlessly into between pillow and pillowcase. It was time to go. The kitchen was still quiet enough that I could hear the front door creak. As I opened it, I turned around one last time and Polimony was still reading at the table, her face as expressionless as before. "So you're not coming with?"

She said nothing and flipped a page.

The public monorail consisted of two nonstop loops, suspended two stories high, circling the center of the city. The orphanage was only two stops and a walk via the blue line. It wouldn't take long to get there. Considering that the closest stop was only a ten-minute walk away; I'd probably be early to tonight's meeting. This was assuming that, A:

Rachel was correct in her implication of 'midnight', and B: I was correct about everything else. A row of red-line cars screeched to a stop behind me and a dozen or so average looking people stepped off. None of them seemed to pay me any mind. It was odd, but I couldn't shake the feeling that someone was watching me. It wasn't something that I felt often, and it had my heart racing like I still had a bag of diamonds in my pocket. I tried to think happy thoughts as the long-awaited blue-line cars came to a stop in front of me. It was probably just a little anxiety about the meeting tonight. Only a handful of people stepped off the blue-line. I waited for them to clear and reached for my flask, unscrewing the lid as I boarded. Automatic doors shut behind me and the standard warnings played overhead. My eyes darted about. Liquor had done little to calm the odd onset of paranoia. The feeling clung to me like wet clothes. I mentally assessed the few people in my car. A homeless person sleeping, a very thin middle-aged woman who looked much too awake, and a man in a gray hoodie diligently texting someone. I dismissed the homeless man and the woman; one was unconscious and the other was clearly preoccupied with everything but me. That left the man in the gray hoodie. We made weird eye contact for a split second before he quickly went back to staring into his cellphone. His thumbs didn't stop moving for most of the ride. Eventually the cars stopped and everyone else stepped off. No one got on. It was just me, him, and an unconscious homeless man. The prerecorded message played again. The audio always ended by suggesting we hold onto the railing, but there wasn't any need for that. The acceleration was so gradual that if it weren't for the windows you might not even know you were moving. Yet I still found myself reaching for something all the same. Gray Hoodie continued to endlessly type. We went the entire next segment of our journey without making any more weird eye contact. As the things outside began to sharpen from a blur, I unwrapped myself from the car's metal pole. My nerve had almost passed as the doors opened and I disembarked, but

Gray Hoodie surprised me by getting off at the same stop. My heart pounded as I went down the stairs and looked over my shoulder. I half expected to see him following me but all I saw was the back of his head slowly sinking beneath the steps opposite. I let out a sigh of relief. There was nothing on this side of town; the station was empty, and I was alone as I made my way down a long dark stretch of concrete.

Within a short walk, the orphanage was well within view. My ears perked, another set of footsteps gradually trailed me, slightly out of sync with mine. I resisted the urge to look back, neurotically scrambling for an appropriate response. After a few panicked seconds of faking a normal walk, I realized why they were out of sync; it's because whoever was behind me was walking slightly faster than me. There was a streetlight a dozen paces ahead. I waited until I reached it then turned around as fast as I could, heart pounding, ready to go all out. I was immediately relieved of this. It was Polimony.

I know, I know. I wasn't mad enough to not worry. And I did start to miss you.

I smiled, elated that it was really only her. "Well, be cool alright?"

Polimony scrunched her nose at my lame comment and smiled. Until then, I had no idea how much I'd missed her too.

We walked side by side now, towards a park bench across the street from the orphanage. We stopped and waited. Even from here it was apparent how deeply the structure had fallen into disrepair.

"How could such a derelict place care for children?"

Rachel's voice answered from behind us. "It doesn't."

She hopped over the bench, her body displacing Polimony's as she sank into the spot beside me. "There are group homes now, foster families. Anything but that."

Polimony readjusted herself, Rachel now in between us.

Rude.

Rachel's eyes met mine as I stared at her in shocked disbelief.

She must have thought I was surprised about her statement rather than her sudden appearance, so she continued, "that building has been shut down for over ten years, but the Historical Society has done everything they can to keep it from being demolished or even repurposed."

I blinked slowly then nodded my head. It wasn't just her appearing seemingly out of thin air that had me drawn in, there was also no one else here. "Rachel,"

She beamed and tilted her head slightly, "uh huh?"

I awkwardly cleared my throat. With her short series of movements, my surprise had somehow been replaced by nervous attraction. "Ah, yes, where is everybody?"

Rachel dramatically looked around and feigned sudden shock, as though she wouldn't have noticed had I not said something.

She kept doing this for what seemed like an entire minute before suddenly laughing out loud at her own bad acting. "No one ever attends these meetings. So far you're the first potentially clairvoyant person I've met. In this town."

She punctuated the last statement with a glance towards my muse. My heart sank, I still hadn't told Polimony about the weird interaction between Rachel and I at *Loretta's*. Polimony immediately began glaring at her.

This was already starting to stress me out, "Well, I'm here. What do we talk about?"

With absolutely no warning, Rachel started placing thoughts into my head again, *Hello? Do I have to think of everything for you? Placing thoughts takes effort for me, I don't do this a lot.*

An uncomfortable tingle traveled down my spine. "What do you mean?"

Rachel sat straight and looked at Polimony, appearing to think for a moment before relaxing again and sending me another thought. *So... Is it just your friend that can read minds?*

Polimony cut her eyes to me then back at Rachel.

Simon?

At this point, I couldn't even tell who was talking; or thinking. Rachel and Polimony exchanged a series of looks before abruptly standing up as if to leave. I wasn't even given a chance for anything to register before another thought came in, possibly from Rachel.

Simon, I think we should move this meeting to somewhere else more comfortable. I have a lot to explain, and a lot to figure out. Do you mind?

I looked at Polimony and she nodded her head, expressionless again.

"Sure. That's fine..."

VI

There was something about being with someone else that made me feel sane. For some reason, spending time with my muse didn't do that for me. It's unfortunate because she's the only person in my life who's convinced me that she cares. Being aware of this has only plagued me with some form of abstract guilt. A kind of looming dysphoric cloud that keeps me from connecting with anyone else. Polimony and I definitely aren't as close as when we first met.

But still, she's the closest person to me.

I don't know that she'd have it any other way.

...

A mildly pleasant organic funk permeated Rachel's small studio apartment. A kettle hissed on an electric stove top, tucked away in a corner kitchenette. The hissing was silenced as Rachel prepared two cups of tea for us. Off to the side, a small antique television faced a twin sized mattress with dark blue sheets. The walls bore simple and colorful modern art pieces. Polimony and I sat separately, facing one another. Polimony made herself comfortable in a maroon recliner while I sank into a modest gray love seat. Both pieces of furniture were situated in the center of the room, a wooden coffee table wedged between them. This could've been my dream apartment if it weren't a studio. Off white carpet muffled each of Rachel's footsteps as she walked towards us. She balanced two steaming mugs as she sat beside me. I nervously fidgeted, worried that we were too close, and hesitantly scooched away. Rachel handed me a mug and readjusted herself, refilling the gap between us and making my heart skip. I quietly sipped at my tea, burning myself in the process. I struggled to hide the pain that sub-boiling water causes when you continue to drink it. There was nothing for me to say, but I still didn't want to shoulder the burden of speaking first. So I continued to burn my mouth with fresh tea.

Rachel set her mug down, laughing as she noticed my poorly hidden grimaces. "I didn't realize you liked tea that much," she looked at Polimony. "Do you want any tea?"

Polimony stared at her with the same searing anger as before.

No.

Rachel nodded her head, smiling as I set my mug down beside hers. "Well, I can make you a courtesy cup. I don't mind at all. I'm glad you're here."

What do you want?

Rachel put her hands in her lap and looked down for a moment before responding. "I have a lot to tell you both. I was planning on just telling Simon about all of this, but now there are two of you! I think the first thing I want to know is *your* name."

My muse shifted in her seat and answered.

Polimony.

Rachel beamed, completely oblivious to the tension that was slowly building in the room.

I quickly interrupted before she could ask Polimony any more questions, "What were you planning on telling me, erm, us?"

"Sorry! I have been looking for another clairvoyant person for a couple years now. I have no idea where to start, I need to go get some things, I'll be right back."

She sprang off the couch, rushing to the kitchen and opening a lower drawer that sounded packed with paper. When she returned she held an intimidating stack of documents. Newspaper clippings, copy paper, maps, and drawings, all this and more were soon scattered across the coffee table. I plucked a corner of stray newspaper out of my tea, flattening it out to dry. Rachel frantically analyzed the mess she had just made, searching for a place to start. Polimony began to intently study everything that had been laid out.

I was a lot more interested in studying Rachel. "A couple years? Why just a couple years?"

She continued to thumb through newspaper clippings. "That is when this started for me. Before that, things were pretty normal. I even had a regular job; I wasn't just living off of disability income."

"Disability income?"

"At first it was terrible; people would be thinking all around me and I had no control over what I could hear. I was committed a few times, medicated, I went through the wringer before I started to get a hold of my new abilities."

I nodded my head, "But, the disability income?"

"Until I figured that out, I was incapable of doing anything. All I could do was search for my mind; I definitely lost it for a while. By the time I *did* figure things out, I had lost everything. It took a year or so, but I had an old friend help me through the process of applying for disability income."

"So, you don't work?"

Rachel scoffed, "Yes Simon. I don't have a job. Are you happy?"

"I didn't mean it like that. I'm just curious what you do all day."

A devious smile formed on her face. "And why's that?"

Polimony cleared her throat, still scanning the mess in front of us.

What is the 'City Gentleman's Club?'

Rachel's ears perked up, arranging a few final scraps of paper. "Okay, first let me fill you in with some foundational knowledge. So, as of right now I have deduced that *Polimony* is clairvoyant, and Simon," the mention of my name distracted me from a sudden troublesome thought, "you're sort of just a lemon. Which is fine! Your arrangement is actually very fortunate: you don't attract nearly as much attention."

Polimony glared at Rachel, now as puzzled with her as annoyed,

Attention?

Rachel smiled, putting a finger in the air. "Have a look at these articles."

She gestured towards two. One read 'Lucky local: Man steals fifteenth straight poker win' , the next read 'Daniel Hudson, aged 35, found asphyxiated in garage from apparent suicide'. The clippings were dated a couple weeks apart. The men pictured in both looked strikingly similar.

Her eyes danced as she noticed the detail register within me. "That is the same man."

But that wasn't why his picture bothered me.

Rachel continued, "how does one win at that many poker games in a row? Asphyxiated in his garage? Suicide? I know it's morbid but it's obvious what happened."

I examined the two newspaper clippings closer. "Someone killed him, is what you're saying?"

Rachel nodded her head and pulled a third article from behind the last: 'Home of sudden poker star burned and leveled over night...'

Before I could say anything, she revealed two more articles: 'Fortune teller dies in shop fire' , 'City police unable to comment on loss of evidence'. Article after article, the same narrative. A dozen or so people dead in fires, over the course of about a decade.

Rachel had arranged them in a timeline, careful to include articles evidencing police inaction. "All the victims were clairvoyant, but why would police suspect that? A poker prodigy, a fortune teller, a prosecutor. To any layman they're just random arson victims, sometimes seperated by two years or more."

Polimony sat still, silently listening with a flat expression. "Over a dozen 'eccentric' individuals dead from the same thing. Not a lot of people *die* from arson in this city. You're looking at the last hundred years of 'suspicious deaths by fire', all occurring in the past ten."

I shook my head in total disbelief. "What? You're telling me no one was burned alive for eighty years?"

"No, what I'm saying is that all of the *suspicious* deaths, *by fire* specifically, started happening about ten years ago."

She placed one last snippet in front of me. It was dated a few months before the article about the poker player: ' Local City Gentleman's Club formed by members of Historic Society.'

"There have probably been a hundred oddly lucky people in the history of this town. They didn't start burning alive until after this group was founded."

I picked up the snippet. A crisp black and white picture of around twenty odd men stood in front of the local orphanage wearing formal attire. I rubbed the deceptively thick paper in between my fingers. She'd reprinted these. My heart fluttered warmly; the thought of manic Rachel hunched over a bunch of microprint at a library was adorable.

I tried to push the feeling aside. "So there's a snooty club in town that kills suspected mind readers?"

Rachel shook her head. "This is only a local chapter, and they have existed for a long time."

She pulled a handful of printed copy paper from beneath the pile of newspaper clippings. "I pulled these from a few other cities, all in different districts: building permits issued to the same 'Gentleman's club' as here. And, in each city that a permit was issued, the same thing happens. Local readers and oddballs start getting burned alive."

I poured over the copied permits, a few of them dated back fifty years. They were all cities within our state, Polimony and I had actually lived in most of them for a time. Recalling that made my spine tingle, the sensation kicking me back into the present. Beneath each permit a few more articles would be stapled, each describing an arson case resulting in death and destruction of evidence. Rachel opened her mouth to elaborate, but then Polimony chimed in, surprising both of us.

It looks like it's only successful 'readers' that end up in the fire.

Rachel jumped slightly, shaken by the unexpected interruption. "I was getting to that, and yes that's partially it. I think they mostly target anyone who brings attention to clairvoyants as a whole. I have a few people in mind that I think might be members, but so far none of them appear to have any abilities. That's why I think it's a sort of secret police. To protect us from ourselves, if that makes sense?"

"If they aren't clairvoyant, then how can they tell who is?"

"Some of their victims recently came into wealth or some other kind of fortune before being burned. As for the others, I think they have some internal clairvoyant people that help find them. I can't imagine a motivation besides blackmail, and I don't think any non-clairvoyant people can read minds. Believe it or not, most people can't even sense when they're being read. Some can sense being read, but they can't read you back. That's why you confuse me. You only get the thoughts that I place, and you can't seem to place or read any. But, I felt you reading me." She gestured towards Polimony before continuing, "Now I'm one-hundred percent sure it was actually Polimony who has been reading me."

I sank further into the cushions of the love seat, unable to hide the anxious confusion that kept crashing into me.

Rachel shot an accusing look at Polimony. "It doesn't really make any sense, unless... Is Polimony a traveler?"

Polimony shrugged.

I sighed. "What's a traveler?"

"Was she, is she like a ghost or a spirit?"

I couldn't answer because I didn't know.

Fortunately, Rachel was perceptive enough to pick up on how lost I was. "Oh... well that's fine. I think I just about went over everything... Do you know what to look out for?"

The question was directed towards both me *and* Polimony.

Polimony cocked her head to the side.

Why should we be on the lookout exactly? If we aren't drawing attention anyway?

Rachel stood up and paced back to the kitchenette, placing the kettle back on the stove. "Well Simon is definitely a great red herring for anything you do, and to anyone who looks further it just looks like you're haunting him. Besides that, you've both probably been seen with me a couple times. We were actually just in front of one of their main meeting places –"

My heart started to race. "Wait, wait, the orphanage? You arranged to have our *secret* meeting directly in front of their hideout!?"

Rachel giggled as she came back over to pick up our mugs. "They weren't having a meeting when we were there silly. And that is definitely not their *hideout*. They have another building an entire ward over. I thought it would be a little funny is all. An inside joke, kind of like a 'screw you' to them."

I shook my head as the kettle began to hiss again. "I don't even know where to begin, why would you do that? Why are you handing out pamphlets if there is a secret organization that kills the *obviously* clairvoyant people? Why aren't you being *less* obvious?"

Rachel moved the kettle off of the burner and prepared two new cups of tea. "Don't get so worked up Simon, didn't you read it? It's a scarecrow. It has very little information by design. Most of these people aren't gifted like us Simon. The few that might be, I haven't run into. As far as I know, they're a bunch of misinformed and paranoid arsonists that set people and businesses on fire. Thanks to my pamphlets they think there is some equally large elusive society of clairvoyants that are bold enough to openly recruit. It might be the only reason my apartment hasn't burned down. That, and the switch to electric appliances and inflammable flooring and furniture."

Polimony rolled her eyes.

I've had enough of this. Rachel, it was nice meeting you but I don't feel like being here any longer. Simon, you need to get better taste in women.

And with that, she did another disappearing act.

Rachel sat down next to me holding two new mugs of tea, a rejuvenated expression on her face. "That was rude, but I didn't really invite her in the first place... Are you sure she isn't a traveler?"

"I have no idea. She's been in my life for as long as I can remember, which isn't very much come to think of it.

"Oh." Her green eyes stared directly into mine as she sipped her tea, "Better taste in women?"

My stomach began doing back flips. I was going to kill her. Polimony could be so inconsiderate when she was angry or bored. "Forget it, she's just mad and being crappy. I should probably go. Now that she's away."

I began to stand up but Rachel grabbed my arm. "No, I want *you* to stay. And now that she's gone you can explain your relationship with her."

I sat down again. My heart began to race as I recalled the initial reason for meeting Rachel. If I wanted anything to come of this I would have to open up. "There's not much to explain. I can't really recall when she first came into my life, but she's been great company. She's also helped me through a lot of tough times. I think it was really bad a few years ago, a lot of trouble at home."

Her voice was softer now when she spoke, "Trouble at home? Bad ex?"

I nodded, hoping the lack of elaboration would come off as cool and mysterious. Though it was sad that a year of misery could be summed up with only two words. "A *really* bad ex."

"I'm sorry that you had to go through that. If it makes you feel better, I know what it's like to look for something in the wrong place. It's hard to let go, and it's almost worse than the search itself."

I sat with that for a moment before asking, "Do you ever feel like you're missing something?"

Rachel smiled, a completely new attitude presenting itself in Polimony's absence. "The way you two interact, It's easy to tell what *you're* missing. Is Polimony helping you out with any *trouble* right now?"

I coughed, choking on lingering droplets of tea. "No! No trouble in my life right now. Not that kind at least."

"You don't get a lot of time without her, do you? I noticed she wasn't around at Loretta's the other day. Did you really stop by because of the pamphlet?"

My mind spun like a prize wheel, a dozen possible responses running through it, each one a blur that overlapped with the rest. "Well I did want a coffee. And the pamphlet was super vague. I wouldn't have been able to figure it out without the poem."

Rachel shook her head, "Simon I think of 'where and when' every time I hand a pamphlet out. I can tell when I'm being read too. She knew."

There's a certain feeling you get when you're being told something that can't fit into your current worldview.

"Why wouldn't she tell me?"

Rachel shrugged her shoulders, quickly changing the subject. "I don't think she likes me very much, but I'm really happy we ran into each other. I'm even happier that you met with me tonight. I'm also really happy that she left us alone for a while. I don't meet a lot of people like me."

I was bouncing back and forth between stunned confusion and anxious excitement. The emotional dissonance froze me in place. She set her tea on the table and placed her hand on mine. There was no time to doubt what was happening as Rachel leaned in towards me. "You don't have to say anything, I can read minds, you know."

For the first time in a long time, I didn't feel alone.

ACT II

VII

I used to have nightmares. Graphic lifelike images of oblivion that I would often confuse with reality. The beginning of these nightmares coincided with the starting or stopping of my lesser habits. As I'd fall deep enough into them they would eventually subside; replaced by the peaceful absence of dreams entirely. I couldn't recall how I fell asleep most nights.

That first night in Rachel's bed, the last thing I remembered was holding onto her as the world drifted away around us. I slept soundly that night.

...

I woke up to the sound of grease popping, breakfast smells filled the room. Rachel had apparently woken up before me and began cooking. As I opened my eyes, light blue plaster filled my vision. Her ceiling was the same color as the day lit sky. I noted this, then rolled over and immediately fell out of her bed with a heavy thud. Laid out on the floor for a little while, I took a disoriented moment to appreciate where I was. It was weird waking up to her. It was weird waking up in her apartment. It was weird waking up in her bed. I closed my eyes, taking everything in and falling into a sort of blissful trance. This was the right kind of weird.

When I opened them up again Rachel was hovering over me, a spatula in her hand and a huge smile on her face. "Not a morning person, I take it?"

The off-white carpet cradled my bare feet as I sprang upwards, my face landing dangerously close to hers. "Not usually. Did you paint your ceiling?"

She chuckled and planted a kiss on my lips before going back to the kitchenette.

Her voice seemed to float through the air towards me, "It gets old, you see the same white canvas every time you look up in almost any interior space. This makes me feel like I'm outside."

"Do you ever consider adding clouds?"

"Right now it's open, I don't have a ceiling. There's nothing above us. Not even clouds."

I stifled a laugh, "They're hard to get just right."

"You paint a lot of clouds?"

My stomach churned when I thought to mention what I did for a living. "Sometimes."

"Hmm."

The air in her apartment was warm. Rachel flipped an egg on the stove and started to whistle. As she stood over the stove I noticed that all she had on was a comically over-sized sweater. My eyes fell to the ground and I smiled. It was *my* comically over-sized sweater. I threw on my pants and tried to squeeze into her shirt, hoping to get a laugh. The shoulders stretched awkwardly and the sleeves quickly tore at the edges. The sudden sound of ripping caused Rachel to spin around mid-tune.

My heart sank. "I thought it would be funny..."

She smiled and turned back to face the stove. "Guess you don't get to leave with a shirt."

"Guess I'll never leave." Damnit, that was bad.

She began to laugh, "Don't make me hold you to that!"

A bit of happiness ran through me again. There was something endearing in the way she laughed. She wasn't laughing at me, but also not with me. Rachel seemed like one of those people who were always passively amused at the world around them. She seemed pleasantly disconnected in our few encounters. The crackling and popping that had filled the morning slowly subsided. A comfortable quiet took its place, broken a few times by the clatter of dishes and silverware as Rachel filled two plates. I waddled over to the love seat, shirtless, sinking once more into what had quickly become my spot. Within a night, I already felt at home. She sat beside me, our breakfast clattering on the wood of the coffee table. Two eggs and two slices of bacon arranged in a cliché smiley face.

"You know, I don't make food for everybody. Don't think this is a regular thing!"

I picked up a fork. Memories of began to replay in my head. "This doesn't feel real."

Rachel dug into her food, unfazed by what I'd said. "It's not supposed to. If it did you'd probably be unhappy."

I had no idea how to take that, so I simply started eating.

She finished her breakfast before I'd made it through a single egg, picking up the conversation through a mouthful of bacon. "You overthink things too much, you don't have to do that around me. Actually, please don't." She pointed to her head and chuckled.

"I actually forgot all about that."

"That's good! Keep forgetting about it! But actually, I wanted to remind you this morning, there are some new plans I have and I wanted to share them with you. But they can wait until after breakfast."

I choked on my second egg. "I've lost my appetite."

Rachel's voice took on a tone of enhanced remorse, "I'm sorry, I didn't mean to make you uncomfortable. I don't purposely read your thoughts, I promise I won't pry. And anyways, you can tell when I do, see,"

My body shook as a tingle shot down my spine, presumably from her.

"You notice it a lot better than most actually, so don't be so paranoid! I'm not like that I swear!"

That wasn't it. But I'd already forgotten what had bothered me. "...You promise?"

"I *promise* I *swear*, how about that?"

"That sounds more than fine."

There was something about her that absolutely disarmed me. I was debating whether or not I was comfortable enough eating alone in her presence, when I heard a wrapper crinkle. She'd gotten an oatmeal bar from G-d knows where, and had begun slowly eating it beside me. Even when she wasn't reading my mind, she read my mind.

As I swallowed my last bite of bacon, Rachel scarfed down the rest of the oatmeal bar. She grinned widely, an oat stuck to her lower lip. I got up to put my plate in the sink but Rachel stopped me. "Don't worry about that, I've been dying to tell you my new idea!"

And then I'd remembered what had bothered me before. I'd only known her four days, but I already suspected that whatever idea she had would make me uncomfortable. "...An idea?"

"I have been running in place for years. There's a lot of information in my drawer, a lot of connections I've made between the Gentleman's Club and various cases of arson and arguably homicide, but I haven't actually thought of anything to do about it."

I sucked my lips into my mouth.

"Stop making that face."

"This is usually the part where someone reveals an awful plan. Don't you watch television?"

"Not reall, but hear me out, I have been looking for another gifted person for a long time. You showing up... I feel like it's a sign."

She had been getting closer to me with each word. Despite the worry I felt, my heart leapt over itself in the delight of being nearer to her. The body didn't know any better. I tried to overcome the sensation, doing my best to maintain a serious tone despite the excitement, "A sign of what? Do you have a plan then?"

Her thigh bumped into mine. "...No, but isn't that a problem? Shouldn't I have one?"

The room had somehow grown quieter, as if it had begun to listen to our conversation.

"Are you sure you've researched everything?"

A wooden sound creaked out of the love seat as Rachel turned beside me. "Simon, I really want to do *something*. You saw the articles. What if something happens to me? Or you and Polimony for that matter."

"Isn't knowing enough? We know what not to do. Wasn't that the point of all your research?"

She picked up her oatmeal bar wrapper and began to fidget with it.

I cleared my throat. "It seems like they're just keeping things under control. They're your – *our* – secret police of sorts. That doesn't sound very malicious."

"They burn people! Alive! Like we're witches or something! And, now that you mention it, there have to be cases where they burned someone on suspicion alone. I know it's happened but I need to make a trip to the library, then you'll see. Are you doing anything this week?"

The portrait. "Ah, yes, erm, I'll be doing things around the apartment but I can make time for this."

Rachel nodded and stood up, slowly walking towards her spooky arson drawer. "You better call me Simon."

I watched as she rifled through papers, the bottom of my sweater barely above the back of her knees. I took a mental snapshot and tried to hold onto it for later recollection.

A tearing sound emanated from the kitchen followed by the tinkling of porcelain. There was the sound of rushed writing and then another tear before Rachel returned.

She planted a pen and two shreds of paper on the table, one written and one bare. "Do you have a phone?"

The love seat creaked once more as I leaned forward, eagerly inking my telephone number on the blank shred. "I do, is this one yours?"

Rachel tilted her head at me and smiled, "No, it's my aunt's. Yes, that's *my* number."

I pocketed the slip of paper and stood to leave.

"Oh, and Simon,"

Rachel made sure to make eye contact before she continued,

"Nobody should have to hide who they are for somebody else's sake."

When I returned home I was wearing my jacket with no shirt underneath. It turned out Rachel was serious about keeping my sweater. The apartment was dark and silent, but I knew Polimony was waiting for me before the lights were on. A flip of a switch revealed my muse, leaning against the counter, sulking.

Fun night out?

The words stung with contempt. "Yes. Fun night in?"

Polimony dredged through the tension to the table, sinking into her usual chair.

She took a deep breath but I cut her off. "Before you say anything, I think she's really nice and different from any girl I've been with."

My preemptive explanation was met with a frown and a pout.

They always are, aren't they?

"Stop that, you weren't there. She made breakfast and we exchanged numbers."

Aw, that's adorable. I am so. Happy. For you.

I took off my shoes and headed into the bedroom in search of a proper shirt. I'd left the heat on and the usually welcoming warmth of the apartment was threatening to suffocate me.

Where are you going?

"I'm getting a shirt, and trying to ignore your negativity."

The familiar clatter of hangers brought a short lived peace as I briefly lost myself in the closet. Eventually I found a nice shirt, shedding the jacket and tossing it on the bed. Polimony was waiting, her mood unchanged.

That's my side. I don't want her smell on my side.

I let out an exasperated exhale, "Why are you being like this? Why can't I like her just because you don't? Aren't you happy that I've met someone who has passions like me? She painted her ceiling, did you notice that before you left? Isn't that cool?"

No, I didn't notice. I was too busy trying to wrap my head around her stupid conspiracies.

"Stupid? What makes you– "

This time Polimony cut me off as I donned a purple button up.

And furthermore, I've talked to her too. She's not that special. She's pushy and fakes positivity. I know you well enough to see another heartbreak when it's coming. I'm going to have to fix it, like always.

My voice shook with frustration, "You have no idea what you're talking about. There was no need to say that, just because you're afraid you won't have anyone else to entertain you."

Entertain me? Really? That's what you think this is?

I sat on the edge of the bed and reached into my pillow case for the diamonds. "I don't know what this is. I didn't think you'd get this worked up over her."

What did you expect?

"I don't know. But do I deserve this?"

Polimony moved beside me and stared at the bag as I caressed it.

I just don't want you getting hurt. I'm so sick of watching other people hurt you.

I tugged at the lace, opening the bag and feeling the coarse bits of diamond inside flow around my fingers.

The smooth silk of the bag and its rough contents pulled away at my frustration. "I know. And you're usually right. I hate that about you," she smiled when I said that, "But I stand by what I said. I deserve the chance to give this a chance. I'm sorry if I've been preoccupied with someone else, it can't be helped."

Polimony put on an awful grin, obviously pleased to hear a rare apology.

I forgive you. I'm sorry about ambushing you this way, but I can't have you forgetting the past so easily. But... You have my blessing. Rachel is officially on my probation.

I laughed, wiping my hands against the inside of the bag before closing it again. "Probation? Your blessing? I don't recall asking for it but I'm glad you're giving us *both* the benefit of the doubt, for once."

I give you the benefit of the doubt every day, your dating life is only the tip of the iceberg.

I shrugged away her comment and placed my apparently Rachel-scented jacket onto my side of the bed.

My hand bumped into my flask in the process. "Aha! Excellent!"

I tore the metal container from the pocket and shook it, eagerly feeling for the weight of precious alcohol. Hollow, of course. Within moments I had the liquor cabinet open and my favorite bottle out.

"This is a special occasion, I didn't drink the entire time I was with Rachel."

Polimony clapped slowly.

Congratulations. And why's that?

"I didn't have the urge. Waking up was a bit rough but it wasn't that bad."

That's great Simon.

I picked up the bottle before filling my flask. The rounded glass was cool against my lips as a familiar burn seared the inside of my mouth.

"I think it's time to break ground on the new project, Hooray!"

Polimony walked to the kitchen table and manifested a book.

Hooray.

When I'd finished the last portrait, I made sure to leave everything ready for the next. This meant that when I looked under the bed, there was a fresh canvas wrapped beside my old easel. When I opened the freezer, my old pallet was still inside. It was one of the few times I interacted with that appliance. The bag I'd brought from Marcus' had various autumn hues and blues in acrylic and oil, along with a washed set of brushes. Everything was quickly laid out on the table. Of course, a glass of liquor and soda found it's way in the mess. Polimony flipped at her book, this time the pages populated with words. Wood scraped at tile as I pulled out a chair adjacent to her. Now I was half in the bag looking at all my supplies, confused.

Well, what are you waiting for?

My gaze bounced between the silk bag and the tubes of paint. "I don't know where to start."

Polimony giggled.

Did you forget what you were doing?

"No, it's not that. I just can't stop thinking about the subject."

Isn't that a good thing?

"Usually, but I'm not thinking about painting."

Well, start thinking about painting.

I couldn't argue with that. "I think I need to clear my head. What day is it? Is Marcus' shop open?"

I'm pretty sure it's open during the week. Wait, clear your head? Isn't that why you're drinking?

I stifled a burp. "It's to keep my brush hand steady and for focus. You wouldn't understand. And, if I'm going to take a break to clear my head I want to go somewhere productive."

Polimony scrunched her nose at me.

Productive? There's a difference between clearing your head and procrastinating. You just want to brag to him about last night.

"There's that. And I'm in the mood for the usual."

That's not happening.

"I still want to go."

You'd really take the bus both ways just to brag?

It was too late, I already had on a coat with the flask stowed in the pocket. "Absolutely!"

The familiar sound of Marcus' shop bell jingled behind me as I staggered in. Polimony crept behind me.

Marcus was by a shelf of brushes, assisting a pale woman with artificially blackened hair. "I understand flat brushes are *aesthetic* I really do miss, but a rounded tip –"

My body slammed into the front counter, bumping the register, and somehow causing the cash drawer to open.

The sudden commotion caused Marcus to whip around, a set of round tip brushes dropping to the floor as he saw the state I was in. "Excuse me miss, while I attend to another customer," He turned back towards her, "I'll be right back, what was your name again?"

I sluggishly reached around the register, trying to close it.

The woman darted her eyes between Marcus and I. "Yeah, Robin, uh, I think I'll come back another time."

Marcus looked after her longingly as she darted out of the shop. She had been the only customer inside.

He slowly spun back around and watched my continued struggle to 'fix' the register. "Simon! You are really fucking me over right now buddy. But, I'm happy to see you're doing well, friend. Finally working on the next masterpiece I see? What can I do for you?"

He lumbered over, easily clicking the drawer shut.

I leaned back against the counter, steadying myself before speaking. "It's going great! But there's a problem. The painting Mark. What. The fuck. Do I do?"

"What do you mean friend? Do what you always do."

My words began to slur out of me, "No, I can paint. But, the girl, she's all I can think about."

"What happened buddy? Are things with your new *bih*– you're new lady, not doing good? You know, I've seen despair fuel your best work this isn't as big a set back as you –"

"NO! It's not like that at all, it's the opposite. Things are going great, way better than with any other *bitch*. Her and I are going to go on adventures!"

Polimony was still cautiously hovering nearby as I continued to lose and regain balance.

This is going wonderfully awful...

I was completely numb to her presence at this point. The bus-drinks had begun to overpower my tolerance. "We're going to bust a secret club or cult or something, Mark. They kill people, they burn 'em."

Marcus shook his head. "My friend, I've seen you in gutters. But a woman? You are good about shaking them off but you are whipped again!"

"Whipped? I only slept with her once."

His head shook again, slower this time. "For you, it is all it takes. Just once."

"I think I'm in love."

Marcus let out a booming laugh that seemed to shake my sight. "In love? I believe you love her but I don't think you are in love. This is worse than I thought my friend, did you tell her about her portrait?"

"No."

"Good, good, You should wait... Do you need more supplies? *The usual?*"

Polimony shot me a death glare serious enough to strike me through my stupor.

I placed an exaggerated hand on my chin, stroking an imaginary beard in thought. Nope, nothing. Marcus watched, slightly disappointed, as I reached for my flask and attempted to drain the contents into my mouth. Unfortunately it was already empty, I had finished it on the bus ride and forgotten.

"Simon, old friend... My shop is closing early today. You need a ride home, I think."

My mouth contorted into a shape vaguely resembling a smile before my body drooped to the floor.

I was a lot more drunk than I felt.

VIII

Most people confuse acquaintances for friends. When I first met Marcus I was a hobbyist with a drinking problem. Now, I'm an *artist* with a drinking problem. On it's own it sounds marginally better, but in the context of my past failures it is quite an improvement. In a time when almost nobody believed in me, Marcus did. And, he was willing to do whatever it took to support that belief. That made him a friend.

...

When I woke up it was dark, both in the bedroom and outside. A foul smell filled my nostrils. I rolled over and felt cold plastic crinkle against me. I shifted my attention away from it, the movement of my eyeballs causing an odd sliding sensation in my head. The front of my sweater was soaked in vomit and the wet fabric clung to my clammy skin. As I slumped out of bed, I felt a lag to the sensation of my body. It was further enhanced by a lack of expected pain. The hangover hadn't fully set in. I burnt up what little energy I had slinking into the kitchen. I felt around for two things: the button on the coffee maker and the handle of the liquor cabinet. My insides tingled as I forced a swig of vodka into my body. I wasn't sick enough to reject it yet. With any luck, I wouldn't have to be. A sigh of relief escaped me as stale water dripped through old coffee, the diluted result tinkling against glass. It wouldn't taste good, but it would give me the motivation to make a proper pot.

I sipped at a cup of my homemade half and half, the bittersweet mixture warming my insides. The concoction brightened everything around me, preparing me to tackle the day. It was early; the coffee maker said three in the morning. I had gotten a large share of vomit out of my sweater. In the end, I thought it best to just throw it out. There was no saving something with that much bile caked into it. A warm shower taken shortly after left me feeling renewed. The new sensation carried me to the answering machine. A dim red 'two' glowed on its LCD from across the room. Not only had it stayed on overnight, it had two messages waiting for me! Polimony had finally woken up too, now nursing a cup of tea and drinking it beside me. I pressed play and we listened to the messages.

"Hey-o, this is Simon. Leave it."

"Simon, buddy, you owe me one after today. My car smells like shit. I wiped it down then had it cleaned, it might as well be yours now. You also owe me for the gifts I gave you. You can pay me back for those easily. Stop drinking so much before you visit. My friend, I was very busy putting on the moves when you dropped by. It was a sure thing!"

Polimony giggled,

No, it wasn't

I tried to push the thought of Marcus' car from my mind. Given the state of my once nice sweater, I could only imagine what his car's interior endured. I'd make it up with the portrait. He didn't really care anyway. With the amount he skimmed off the top, he could get it redone. And this was before considering his 'unrelated' business. The machine beeped, and another message played.

"Hey-o, this is Simon. Leave it."

"Hey-o! Hahaha I like that a lot. You still use one of these? Ha ha, I really like that... Anyways, I've been thinking about what we talked about the other night. I'd love to meet soon... And I miss you a little ..."

My ears perked, "A little?"

Polimony hushed me.

"Whoops! Forget I said that! Are you free this Saturday? Call me back when you can! I'm going to be back and forth from the State Office all week but I'll be checking my voicemail! Bye Simon."

There was a final beep followed by silence.

"That's only a couple days away, I figured we'd have longer."

On a deeper level, I'd mentally distanced myself by pretending we'd never see each other again. The concrete plans brought with them a new wave of anxiety.

The message was a bit long as well.

"I'm not nitpicking or anything, but she's using up all my tape."

Polimony snorted.

I feel like that one is on you, Simon. Why are you being cheap about tape? Why are you even using tape? You literally just - "

"I get it, you're still mad about how I spend *my* money."

I'm just saying.

"You're 'just saying' too much. I need to... Do you think it's too early to call her back?"

Does it really matter? If you're playing by 'the rules' though, it's definitely not the right time. You should wait a day or two.

I nodded my head, thinking of what to do next.

Polimony tapped her foot a few times then walked towards the bedroom.

Well, since you're okay, I'm going to sleep on it.

"Why did you come out if you were just gonna go right to bed?"

I was waiting for you to wake up and get out of bed. You were covered in throw up and hogging both sides, now that you're out of bed I can sleep.

My lips formed a pout. Once again, I wasn't sure how to take that. There was nothing to be said, she was right after all.

"Will I see you soon?"

Goodnight, Simon. Or is it good morning? You really need to stop doing this to me."

Polimony stuck her tongue at me and went into the room, leaving me alone. I wasn't sure if I was meant to join her or not. In the moment of indecision I resolved to do nothing, my mind trailing off as I sipped at my drink. There wasn't much time to think before Polimony's voice stabbed at me from the bedroom.

You left your bag in here! And it's on my side!

The grunt that escaped me did zero justice to the annoyance she'd suddenly stirred in me. "Sometimes, I feel like you're a bother for the sake of it. Does it really matter what side you sleep on? You know I would've come to get it eventually."

She giggled and sank under the sheets.

No, it really doesn't matter. I just thought you got off too easy.

"Got off with what?"

No answer. Maybe that was the answer. It could have been a lot of things depending on how far back you went.

I couldn't help but feel giddy as I dumped the contents of the baggie onto the kitchen table. It was like breaking open a pinata, or laying out all your candy after Halloween. My imagination went to Rachel, the thoughts of candy intermixing with her. I made a mental reminder to purchase some. She probably liked candy, lots of women probably like candy. I shook away the thought of her in an attempt to stay focused on the task at hand. We'd been together once and she was already distracting me from my work. An assortment of materials were laid out in front of me. I assessed each one, considering how they would factor into Rachel's portrait. There were various colors of paint, most notably a dozen or so samples of blue. There were a handful of small brushes and sticks thrown into the mix, as well as the diamonds in their little pouch. A warm appreciation filled me as I noticed the latter. Marcus had not only kept the diamonds secure, but he hadn't taken a visible amount out of the bag. The feeling was quickly displaced with a sudden wonder. He mentioned that I'd ruined his car, so he must have given me a ride home. But, did he put me to bed too? My eyes darted about as I pictured my friend tucking me in. I shook my head, it was a strange thought. Crinkling plastic filled the room as I turned the plastic baggie inside out. A note fluttered out, it further detailed Marcus' complaints about yesterday. The note, now balled up, made a wonderfully satisfying thump as it hit the inside of my trash can. I grabbed a bowl and a metal chopstick from the cupboard before returning to the table. An entire tube of sky blue paint made its way in. My hand shook as I reached for the pouch. Nerve threatened to bubble over into panic despite how long I'd planned to do this. A return trip to the kitchen was made and a bottle brought back. The anxiety was soon quelled as that familiar warmth filled my stomach. There wasn't any way to reverse what I was about to do. My heart still pounded as I emptied a portion of the diamonds into the bowl. Just shy of half the bag glittered on top of the paint. I inhaled sharply, picked up the chopstick, and stirred.

The paint completely swallowed the diamonds, rendering the originally glorious luster entirely invisible. A coarse texture was the only evidence that anything was even in the paint. It could have been ordinary sand to anyone else. It felt like every organ inside of me was imploding simultaneously as I stirred harder, thinking that might somehow fix the problem.

I can't say I'm surprised.

"AH!"

I jumped up, somehow knocking the bowl off the table in the process. It shattered as it hit the ground, leaving a crunchy pool of paint contaminated with broken pieces of glass.

Polimony knelt down beside it.

That's unfortunate.

"Why aren't you in bed!? I thought you were going to sleep! Look at this!"

Aren't you glad I'm here to help now?

I gestured wildly at the mess all over the floor. "Help? What? How are you going to help me? Are you going to manifest an intangible broom and dustpan? A mop as well? Perhaps a filter and vacuum?"

I don't think you're getting those diamonds back.

Now I was jumping up and down, blindly dodging the shards of glass with each landing. "Obviously!!! Why do you think I'm so frustrated right now!"

Polimony stared at the mess, tilted her head and giggled.

Have you tried mixing the diamonds with acrylic?

I sat back down, staring off in a trance-like state. Short of jumping out the bedroom window, I'd exhausted all physical expressions of excitement. My body responded by looping back to apparent ease, completely without movement. "What, what are you suggesting right now?"

You should be open to new ideas.

"New ideas? What do you think I just did? Were you here for that or were you still pretending to be asleep?"

Polimony shifted her attention towards me, visibly bothered.

For your information, I was sleeping until you starting clinking around in that bowl like a crazy person. If anyone should be angry right now, it's me.

I inhaled deeply, slowly exhaling for effect. "I just wasted thousands of dollars worth of diamond, and dropped it onto the floor. Now you suggest throwing away the remaining half. And *you're* the one who is mad. You are. Is that right?"

They were thrown away as soon as you considered doing that. What did you think would happen? Was this really your plan?

"They were supposed to sparkle *in* the paint... I didn't think 'in' would become 'underneath.'"

She finally stood up, eyes locked on mine as before.

That's just silly. I figured you'd dust the paint while it was wet.

With that, I stood up to meet her. "Polimony."

Simon.

"Why didn't you say that before I spent thousands on a whole forty grams of diamond dust?"

She shrugged and took on a smug smile.

It isn't my money.

After scraping at textured tile then accepting that the grout line was ruined, the mess was clean and the glass was in the trash. I had scraped up as much diamond paint as possible and put it in a plastic bowl instead of a glass one. The kind you could put a lid on, in case you were afraid of dropping it.

"You know what, I think this was for the best."

Polimony had been sitting at the table, watching me and reading for the past hour.

You could do our grout in blue, then if you did the tiles in white it'd be like we were walking on clouds.

"I'm not in the mood for these sorts of ideas right now. This is the kind of damage that loses someone their deposit."

She scrunched her nose at me.

You say that like it matters. Isn't that one of the reasons you chose this unit? So we didn't have to worry about that?

That, and because it was the first one available when I had to move.

I quickly changed the subject. "Okay, I liked your other idea a lot, it's kind of like glitter on glue right?"

Polimony nodded.

Yeah, it'd be the very top layer.

I traced the bottom of my chin with two fingers, stroking an invisible beard and considering the steps ahead of me. "We have a lot of work to do. Do you know what I did with those leaves?"

The question was met with a laugh,

Hahaha, you mean the compost from last week?

"It's only been a few days, do you recall where I put them?"

No. You never put them anywhere. They were leaves.

"They *are* very important leaves, and they didn't just disappear."

A memory popped into mind and I ran for my jacket.

How long do you think dead leaves last?

Tiny shreds of plant matter rained out of the pockets as I turned them inside out.

"Well darn"

Really? What did you expect? It's like you don't think anything through lately, what's gotten into you?

I lowered my head and threw on the jacket. Bits of dry leaves grazed my hands as I rummaged about the pockets.

"I don't know, I can't think straight."

Polimony pouted and walked to the front door, blocking me from leaving.

It's her. It's always a 'her'.

"As opposed to what? As opposed to whom?"

She said nothing as I continued to fidget with the pockets, eventually noticing that my flask was missing.

"I really am losing it, aren't I?"

You're hopeless.

I made a frantic run of the apartment: filling my flask, stashing the diamonds, and putting the plastic bowl into the freezer – the paint would last longer that way.

"You need to get off my case and cheer up. I know when you're in a funk. Stop being jealous, I thought you were okay with this."

Polimony stood quietly, looking down with her arms crossed.

"Seriously, stop it. Come outside and get leaves with me. I'm not letting you sit in here and sulk."

Finally she walked away from the door and towards me.

You say that like I was going to let you leave alone.

There was suddenly a relaxed attitude about her as she smiled. My chest seemed to flutter as her eyes briefly passed over mine. Blue. I had spent a lot of time trying to forget how Polimony could make me feel.

I'll get ready.

The seasonal cold air that had settled in town surrounded us. It was still early, and this afforded a great opportunity to watch the sun rise. There were a great deal of people out, filling the diners and getting wired before work. Usually the crowds would persuade me to stay inside, but today they did little to dampen my endless desire to waste money. Despite my looming appetite, I didn't want to eat at Loretta's. The charm it held as a niche establishment had begun to fade with repeated exposure. In fact, the thought of dining there almost felt like charity, and not the kind that made you feel good inside. Rather, the kind of empty giving that only served to displace guilt. Or maybe I just wasn't in the mood for lousy coffee. We passed it without further thought.

Polimony started bouncing with each step, quickly leaping ahead of me.

I am in the mood for some place cheap!

"We just passed that, but I'll bite. What did you have in mind?"

She paused, looking up as though deep in though.

I had somewhere in mind... But now I don't

I smiled and shook my head at her. She moved behind me as I continued walking, uneager to stay still for long on such a busy sidewalk.

Let's go somewhere new! I want you to take me somewhere that we haven't been before.

Immediately, I turned around. Polimony froze so she wouldn't run into me face-first.

What's wrong?

"We have to take the bus, for sure. I think we may have eaten at every restaurant in our ward."

Her hair brushed by me as she resumed walking. She soon passed me, becoming the new lead.

Okay then, new rule: Somewhere we haven't been in over a month. And, I remembered where I wanted to go.

"That's a lot easier... The bus is that bad?"

Worse than bad.

I paused as Polimony continued down the sidewalk in front of me. She still hadn't told me what she had in mind; perhaps she was too excited to say. My legs broke into a run after her, the eager curiosity giving way to a blind chase.

After what seemed a dozen blocks, she came to a sudden stop in front of a generic fast-food restaurant. The sign pulled my attention away from her. It read "Andees" in unlit neon. We'd been to one of these possibly a hundred times together, across multiple cities. There was a reason we hadn't been to one in so long, but it had been long enough for me to forget. The memory was bothersome, bothersome enough to invoke a reach for the flask. Polimony turned around, the smile on her face fading into a mixture of disgust and concern.

Can you put that away? No one can see me and yet I'm still embarrassed of you.

I smiled as the much-needed warmth seeped into the cracks of my being. "I'm sorry you feel that way. Personally, I feel great."

If only you saw what I saw.

I buttoned up my jacket, following her inside. "I do, I just don't mind what you see."

Inside, there wasn't much activity. The floors were the same checkered tile as Tony's, but without the crudely drawn bagels on them. The walls were maroon painted plaster with oddly eastern artwork and tapestries. The tables shone the usual glossy black, but they were set in the style of a Chinese restaurant. White fluorescent with yellow covers imitated, as best they could, pleasant lighting from above. Despite the odd choice of decoration, this Andees' maintained the same black and maroon color scheme. The pair was oddly comforting, and kept the franchise familiar no matter how it was furnished. A line of people stretched from the front counter ahead. It wasn't a long line, but it wasn't so short as to keep us from reacquainting ourselves with the menu. Polimony needed to figure out what she'd manifest for herself. I needed to figure out what was actually worth the money. At first glance: nothing. That was probably why it was so affordable. As people finished their orders and turned around to wait, I noticed a striking similarity between all of them: Everyone in the line was Asian; Chinese specifically. I spun around, taking note of all that I could. Everyone sitting down was Chinese. Everyone outside the window was Chinese. Everyone behind the counter was Chinese, save for one sharply dressed Latino gentleman going from station to station. But even then, he yelled at the other employees in what sounded like confident Chinese.

Besides him, Polimony and I were the only non-Asian people immediately visible. I felt uncomfortable, which naturally led to me feeling guilty for feeling uncomfortable.

A middle-aged woman at the register barked at me, snapping me out of my confused guilt. "Hey, you, order now!"

Polimony laughed at me as I tip toed towards the register. The line-gap that I now traversed had apparently grown to be unacceptably large. A mumbled greeting bumped into itself on the way out of my mouth, "M-Mi hao."

The cashier seemed to cringe a little and ignored my failed attempt at assimilating.

She continued in English, "What you want? Rine behind you."

Oh my G-d, I wish I had a camera.

I strained to ignore my muse on top of what I had just said. "Yes, yes... A number seven? And an iced tea, *pur-rease.*"

"You rike the tea in the Andees Mountain Size?"

I had a chuckle, "No, thank-kuh roo? The medium is the fine."

Why are you talking like that? They know enough English to know you're being an ass.

"Mmhmm okay, you number two eighteen. Name?"

"Simon"

"Simon, two eighteen, You wait now!"

Another person in line quickly displaced me, completing a much smoother order in Mandarin while I waited for my food.

"I don't know if I'm going to eat inside or just bring this home."

Polimony was still laughing beside me.

I should bring you here more often.

My foot tapped while the sound of scraping metal and clanking cutlery sounded from behind the counter. I couldn't even be mad, it was my fault for being so distracted. Looking out the front windows of the restaurant, it was obvious that she had led me into a predominately Chinese part of town. Besides street signs, most boards and signage weren't in English. More and more indicators made themselves present, but the realization was randomly interrupted as a woman in the middle of the dining area vomited all over the floor. Then a man moved next to us, also awaiting his order. Everyone turned their attention towards the putrid yellow pile in the center of the restaurant. The smell began to waft around as two young boys holding towels ran out from a side door. They seemed to race each other to the mess, one wiping it up then the other polishing the floor. As they did this, conversations started again and people went back to eating. This included the woman who had just thrown up, she didn't even acknowledge the two boys cleaning the mess beside her.

A paper bag and a white cup appeared next to us with a yell, "TWO EIGHTEEN, SIMON!"

I swiped the bag and ran out the front doors.

Where are we going to eat? They had a booth by the window that I wanted.

My feet struck the pavement as I moved just beneath a jog in search of an open patio.

"We should get some fresh air!"

A crumpled up napkin I'd used to wipe my face made it's way into my now empty paper cup. Shortly after, the paper cup made it's way into a rusty trashcan. I'd eaten everything despite what I just saw, the food was deceptively delicious. In the process, I'd managed to save the paper bag without ruining the inside with any grease.

The paper crinkled as I opened it in the air. "You see Polimony, this was all a part of my plan."

She didn't listen at first, she was too busy eating her food. Unlike me she had the benefit of eating anything I'd ever eaten. If I'd experienced it, she could manifest it for herself. It limited things like reading and movies, but non-specific things like food came with no issues. The ability came in handy when she wanted to avoid eating at a restaurant that she took me to as a joke.

Her ears perked up as she noticed me think of her.

Hmm?

"The bag. In the end, this is what it was all for."

No, no it was not. You forgot to bring one.

"If you knew, why didn't you say anything?"

You were going to end up with one wherever we ate. What restaurant doesn't have bags?

"Whatever. Are you done yet? You're supposed to help me look, I'm waiting on you."

The streets had lost a lot of the previous traffic. The morning rush had ended, and what was left over were outliers: people working odd hours and people who weren't working.

I thought you took me out for my sake, weren't you going to do this on your own?

"Fine. I specifically remember mentioning you helping me, but fine."

Polimony rolled her eyes and threw her trash on the ground.

You're so dramatic sometimes.

I wasn't going to bite that bait, instead I allowed my focus to shift to the subject of my portrait:

Rachel.

"Rachel... So unique and quick to hold my attention. Like this little leaf."

Words flowed forth in near-sing-song as I bent over to pick up a small yellow leaf.

Polimony stayed beside me, her footsteps in sync with mine.

Simon... So eccentric and quick to creep me out. Like a sex predator. Or an obsessed artist, secretly painting a picture of me. One that he plans on selling to strangers.

A breeze picked up, bringing with it another cascade of leaves around us. They almost floated into my hands before being shoved into the paper bag. I made sure to grab less dead ones this time, that way they wouldn't decay into nothing so quickly. A pleasant side effect of my new leaf-picking criteria was that the ones I chose were more colorful. We continued in a fairly constant pattern. A few steps, then a stop. Over and over this continued, with each stop resulting in a leaf or two being placed vigorously into the bag. Polimony didn't seem to mind the constant stopping. She actually appeared peaceful, content almost. It was a calm emotion that I hadn't seen in her for quite some time. A sickness ebbed at me as a fuzzy memory came to mind. The weirdest things would stir them, and at the worst of times. I didn't want to drink though, I couldn't ruin this kind of happiness for her. It wasn't long before the feeling subsided and the bag was almost full. By the time I'd bent over to pick up a final fiery orange leaf, we were only a few blocks from our apartment. We turned and cut through an alleyway back to Main Street. A narrow brick tunnel devoid of people, with a light at the end. The beckoning break in darkness was periodically blocked off by the transient body. The hour had a way of turning the often ominous into proper poetry. The portrait began taking on more detail in my mind. The subject in the center would change in my head each time I imagined it. It was always Rachel, but Rachel wasn't always the same. Her form was as transient as the ever changing body that would block the light at the end of an alley. Though one thing stayed consistent through it all: that dazzling blue skirt. I gripped the paper bag tight. New inspiration sent me running home, crisp air filling my lungs with each short breath. Polimony rushed to keep up. We'd gotten enough leaves, it was time to start painting.

...

Over the course of a few hours I'd set everything up on the table. My easel, palette, brushes, pre-mixed paints, and the plastic container of diamond filled blue paint. For the first hour or so, Polimony had helped me organize each leaf by color, shred them, and mix each with the correct color paint. She had a keen eye for color matching, one I relied on often. I had drawn a dozen rough sketches and shown them to her with mixed results. After an additional hour of pure disagreement, I independently settled on one that was now projected onto a full-sized canvas. After putting everything in place and staging a bottle and some light snacks, everything was ready. The piece would be abstract, but discernibly Rachel. All there was to do now, was paint it.

IX

In the trance of work there was an occasional transition from pinpoint fixation to sudden awareness. Only briefly, could I see the big picture. These occasional episodes of clarity were usually brought on by a lack of sufficient inebriation. They could be used as an informal measurement of time, though I rarely bothered adding them up. Instead, I used them as periods of insight. It created a productive cycle of detailed focus broken by occasional contextual awareness. First it was all about a single item: the shade of this section of the background, the texture here, the form there. Soon, the rest of the painting would come back into view. Then I would have a drink and make another series of corrections.

...

A feeling struck me, the sudden feeling that a significant amount of time had passed. It was enough to snap me out of the trance of work. Regular intake of gin and coffee had helped me stay focused enough to lose track of time in the rhythm of it all. The familiar smell of mineral spirits emanated from the canvas as I put the finishing touches on Rachel's form. Autumn hues, with the flaky texture of crisp leaves, popped out around her. The difference in depth created a sense that she was sinking into the background. I inhaled deeply as I put the brush down in favor of the bottle, exchanging the feeling of cheap wood for cool glass . The smell went away a little more as I set the bottle back down and wiped my mouth. Despite leaving the bedroom window open, the apartment still smelt like I was painting again. Picking the brush back up, I stepped back and looked at the canvas. . She needed to stand out from the background like she did in the real world. Inspecting it one last time, I was certain. It was ready for the final touch.

Polimony crept up behind me, anxious of potentially interrupting me.

Finishing up? Are you going to eat now? It's not like it'll dry soon.

I stared at *Rachel*. Admittedly, not a lot was left to the imagination. "Do you think she'd like it?"

Is she buying it?

Polimony didn't say anything else as I made an inspection of what I'd done so far. Finishing the once over, the feeling came to me again. It was fatigue. The feeling was fatigue. In an instant every muscle in my body began to ache. The air came to life around me. It was cold in our apartment. The lights appeared relatively dim. Orange daylight streamed in from the bedroom window, enough to be visible from the kitchen. I took a deep breath in, and released it. I could almost feel my blood circulating. There was only one thing left to do and then it would be complete. *Rachel* would be complete.

Polimony studied the painting, expressionless.

That definitely looks like her.

The tiles were cool against my back as I stretched out on the floor, weak. "It is her. Almost."

It's okay. It's the process that matters. You're bringing somebody to life. Somebody new.

A darkness began to slowly creep in around the edges of my vision, obscuring my view of the ceiling. "Once the diamonds are added, it *will* be her."

Hmm.

Polimony stood over me, slightly bothered, as the world faded out of view.

Sleep well, Simon.

When the world lit up again, I was still on my back. This time, I had a clear view of the ceiling above. As I sat up, I knocked over a glass of water that had found its way beside me. The mellow late-afternoon orange from the bedroom had become the bright white of day.

Polimony was apparently waiting, cheerful as can be.

Good morning!

The sound of her voice set off a dull beating in my head.

I shooed her away and stood up. "Coffee, liquor, bright."

She backed away as I stumbled to the kitchen, desperate to stop the now pounding headache. My hangover was becoming long overdue, but I only needed to put it off for a little while longer. The portrait only needed one last thing, then there was a phone call to make.

Is it so hard to say 'good morning' back?

My hands trembled slightly as I started a pot of coffee and opened my favorite cabinet.

Within a minute, my headache was fixed. "You know my process."

She folded her arms and stared at me with wholehearted contempt.

"Fine. Good morning, Polimony."

Her frustrated disposition was quickly replaced by the warmth I was woken up with.

There. Was that so hard? Are you excited to finish your project? You've been out of it for a while.

"How long is a while?"

Long enough for you to ask.

"Helpful."

My legs wobbled slightly as they took me towards the answering machine. The small display was once again unlit. I grunted and did the usual routine, angrily unplugging until the display came back on.

"I cannot stand this thing, why do you think it does this?"

Maybe it just hates you. Is the date right?

"Obviously not."

The coffee maker in the kitchen was much more reliable. It diligently displayed the fact that I'd been in a trance for the better part of a week. It was now Saturday morning.

"Fuck."

Polimony laughed as I rushed to the phone and dialed Rachel's number.

Forgot something?

I put a finger to my lips and kept my eyes on her while the line rung. After a handful of rings it went to voicemail.

"Hey this is Rachel, you missed me but feel free to leave a message!"

Reason trickled through panic as I considered hanging up, formulating a proper message, and calling again. A loud beep interrupted the thought, I'd waited too long.

"Hey, hi, it's Simon. Sorry, I've been super busy working... Totally in another world you know. I'll be home all day so call back whenever, I didn't know if you still wanted to come by – I definitely still want you to! I just know it's been a while since you left a message, and I wasn't sure if something might have come up or..."

Polimony's eyes met mine from across the room, her lips puckered.

"Ahem, or something. Anyways, sorry"

I shut my eyes, putting away the receiver and immediately trying to dissociate from the awful message I'd just left.

Wow. That's an awful-lot of tape you just used. Do you think that she'll mind?

"She has a cellphone."

I was being sarcastic. No one but you cares about that.

A ripping sensation went through my stomach. Nowhere in my recollection, of the past several days, was I eating. Nor was I drinking anything besides black coffee or liquor. My shirt dragged along the wall as I slumped to the ground, unsure of how to best take care of my body. "Polimony."

Yes.

She had situated herself at the table with a mug of coffee. Her face had set itself smug in the presence of my suffering.

"I think I'm dying."

My statement was acknowledged by a dramatically long sip, followed by an exaggerated swallow.

Mmm. That's terrible. You should probably do something about that.

"Polimony."

You aren't seriously asking me how to survive in your own apartment, are you? Your apartment that you lease in a first world country? With running water and a microwave?

"No. I want moral support. I don't want to get up."

Then you just die I guess.

Another drawn out sip of coffee.

What a terrible loss.

"You're really good for nothing, you know that?"

The wall kept me upright as I brought myself back to my feet. It had been a while since I'd gotten this lost in my work. I wasn't sure what to eat, and didn't have the energy to go out and let the city decide. In the desperation of hunger, I opened the fridge for the first time in perhaps a month.

Simon, wait -

Out came a smell so revolting that it warmed the air. I doubled over, immediately shutting the door and resealing weeks of apparently forgotten take out.

- The fridge is turned off.

"But the freezer works! Why is it so warm?"

Polimony pouted and crossed her arms.

I just told you, the fridge is turned off. You got angry last month and said you were 'too fancy to eat left overs.' Then you turned our fridge off. Why don't you heat up one of the frozen meals? They last forever.

"Um, no they don't. And wait, why don't I remember doing this?"

Because you have a drinking problem.

A whimper escaped me as I held my nose, cracking open the fridge to see the set of two dials inside. The freezer was set to specification. The fridge was set to zero. Apparently zero meant off.

"Frozen it is."

A muffled cacophony filled the kitchen as I dug past frozen paint supplies and frosted mystery meats. My hand found cardboard. I pulled an old box of fish sticks from the depths of the freezer.

Those are raw.

"So am I."

The rest of the box conveniently fit into a plastic bowl without spilling over. A handful of beeps sounded and the microwave began a ten minute run.

I flipped the box over as the fish sticks cooked. "That's weird, they don't have microwave instructions."

They're raw.

"That's why I'm cooking them."

Polimony shook her head and drank from her mug, staring at the microwave with me.

The oven is right next to you. You've waited several days, what's twenty more minutes?

"I've waited several days. I'm fucking starving."

Then why didn't you just find a microwave meal!

BEEP BEEP BEEP.

"See? The microwave disapproves of what you just said."

You really are starving, you're delusional.

The door opened to reveal a pleasant smelling pile of limp, steaming, fish sticks.

"Finally."

I couldn't wait, as soon as the bowl was on the counter I bit into a chewy stick. "OW!"

Amazing.

Hunger overrode patience and over the course of a minute I repeatedly burnt my mouth, wolfing down chewy bits of fish fillet and soggy breading. Polimony watched me as I put the bowl in the sink, then began drinking as much tap water as I could. In the span of fifteen minutes, I'd sated every immediate need.

Polimony set her coffee mug down, apparently finished.

You did it Simon. You survived.

"The sarcasm is unneeded. I'm just taking care of myself."

The smell of fish surrounded me as I burped. It was actually the first time in a long time I'd had fish sticks without any sauce.

"And, now that I've refueled, I can add the final detail to *Rachel*."

You do that.

Polimony stood up, and brought her empty coffee mug to the bedroom.

"You're really going to miss this? It's the last part, the most dazzling addition, it may actually warrant a proper ceremony."

You really want me to be here for it?

"Of course."

She smiled at me as I tried to mimic her patented pout.

I can't say no to that. Let me get a book from our room first.

"I'll join you! I need to get the final element anyways."

It only took a minute or so for us to reconvene at the table. Her with a book, and me with the last of the diamonds. The easel was waiting, the surface of *Rachel's* oil skirt still shining with moisture. I picked up the still wet brush, dipped it in turpentine, then generously dug around in the pouch with it. When I brought it out it glittered magnificently, exactly as I'd initially imagined. The diamonds adhered perfectly, forming a sandy texture; about half of them being dulled by the thin paint. I wasn't worried though. Being the last thing painted, it would be the last thing still touch-wet. That gave me time to dust it later; like glitter on glue. At this point it was almost finished, but it was already perfect. I could hardly contain my excitement as I rushed to the phone. My fingers quickly punched in Marcus' number. An eager tremble traveled through me. I couldn't wait to hear how he'd take the good news.

The other end rang a few times before he finally picked up. "Simon, how goes it my friend? Are you going to apologize for last week yet?"

It didn't matter, he could have that. I already had this. "Yeah alright, I'm really sorry I fucked up your car. I've been busy -"

"Busy!? Are you close buddy? It's been almost a week since I heard from you last."

"Mark, I'm done. It's finished. It needs one last thing but we can sort that out before the next auction."

"Finished, auction, two of my favorite words to hear from you! I will make some phone calls today! You have been silent for a while buddy, everyone will be very excited to hear your name again!"

My face was beginning to hurt I hadn't smiled this hard in months. "Let me know as soon as you have things sorted. You know I'm not busy. Leave a message, ambush me, write it in the sky, I don't care! I can't wait to be back out there again."

"Of course my friend, I will call you soon!"

This time I was the one to hang up. For the first time in over a year, I was able to shut my eyes and bask in a lack of self-obligation. A celebratory mug of my special half and half was made. It was immediately finished and refilled with another. The wave of dis-inhibition calmed my racing excitement and freed my mind to think. My attention turned to tonight's plans with Rachel. I turned to face Polimony, and sobered my expression slightly. She was reading at the table and smiling peacefully.

"So, where are you going to hang out while Rachel is over?"

Polimony shut her book and looked up at the ceiling, annoyance plastered across her face.

Are you asking me to leave while you have another woman over?

"Well, don't say it like *that*. It's just, I didn't know if she was going to want to spend the night. I want to keep options open."

Out of sight out of mind, huh?

The annoyance turned to disgust as her eyes shifted from the ceiling to me.

I finished the rest of my drink and cleared my throat. "Mmm, yes, pretty much. I'm sorry, it'll probably only be this one time, she hasn't seen my room is all."

Our room. And I'll think about it.

Polimony ended her statement with a certain finality that grabbed hold of me through my nascent buzz. It was a thing that only she could do. She turned her attention back to her book, her face expressionless. I leaned against the counter and made another drink, trying to smooth over the tension that had formed. Then the phone rang, a release from the situation that I'd so quickly created.

I rushed to answer, eager to hear a voice that didn't belong to Polimony or me. "Hello?"

The line crackled a little, I could hear a lot of noise in the background but it wasn't clear what. Soon a voice broke through, Rachel's.

"Hey, Simon? I'm on the way, I know you said five but it'll probably be closer to six. Someone jumped in front of the monorail and they need to clean it up real quick. That's okay right?"

Again?

Never too bitter to pry, I tried to will Polimony away but it didn't work. Her ear was almost adjacent to mine by the receiver.

Rachel was still on the line, waiting patiently while I silently argued with my muse. "Simon?"

I snapped into reality, tightening my grip on the receiver. "Yes, yes, of course that's fine! I can't wait to see you. I miss you too, a little, perhaps."

I slapped myself on the head while Polimony walked away laughing to herself.

How can you enter a building, when you're only good at closing doors?

After a long pause Rachel's voice hesitantly peaked through the line, "... Really?"

My face flushed. I knew without seeing that she was blushing, and it made me absolutely ecstatic. There were no wrong moves with her.

"Absolutely! I'll be home. You have the address right?"

"Oh, of course! By the way, I'll have a little surprise for you too. You didn't make any reservations or anything for tonight did you?"

"No, why? Did you?"

"Nope! Just... Be hungry, is all! I cannot wait to see you Simon." There was a long pause. I didn't want to be rude so I waited for her to hang up, but she continued instead. "Is Polimony there?"

A ruffling came from the bedroom.

"Don't worry, I'm going to take care of that."

"No! It's fine, really! She should be there for the updates on my research." Her excitement chirped through the line, "I have been in and out of the library! A couple of the people at the front desk think I'm insane. Can you believe that?"

I chewed at my lip, unsure if she was joking or not. "No...?"

"You're so funny Simon! I'll see you in a bit. Apparently this guy made a huge mess. Everyone's really mad about it."

"See you then."

There was a small blip on the other end before it went silent. The call was over. I put the receiver away and went into the bedroom, sprawling out on the bed and fixing my gaze on the ceiling above.

A single detail from the odd conversation kept replaying in my head. "I know you said five."

Polimony began to make a clamor in the closet. Hangers clattering, knocks, footsteps, an annoying shower of sounds raining onto me for an unreasonable amount of time.

Finally, I snapped. "What the hell are you doing in there!? Are you alright?"

The racket stopped, and my muse walked out wearing the same exact outfit as before.

Do you think I'm pretty Simon? I don't feel pretty today.

"I don't know why you'd go through the motions of looking for clothes. You can wear whatever you'd like."

What would you like?

All the bitterness of the day had left her tone. All that remained was Polimony's soft voice, unadulterated by sarcasm, anger, or anything else. It was something sweet that I rarely got to hear. That sinking feeling filled my heart again. A feeling of longing that was strong enough to push you away from what you longed for.

Simon?

"I don't know."

Do you still think I'm pretty?

"I ... don't know."

Polimony looked down at the floor for a while. A silence filled the room. The kind that wrapped the people in it for a while; keeping them safe from the burden of speaking. When she finally looked up again, light glinted from each of her eyes.

I'll leave you and Rachel alone tonight.

Something had entered her perfect tone again, something that weighed each of her words to the floor. She stared at me for a moment before vanishing. I couldn't think of anything to say to her anyways. I couldn't even rationalize how I felt. I think I was supposed to feel relieved. It almost felt like nothing at all.

X

Deep within the core of my being was a need to be lost. A need to be somewhere else. In that sense, there was no fixed destination. The endless travel manifested itself as a constant feeling of malaise. When I was still, the entire world was off by a degree, just enough to notice. The only fixed destinations I had were artificial, manifested through a medium – often oil and sometimes acrylic. In the trance of my work, I could be lost exactly where I was.

...

The conversation with Polimony crept in and out of my mind as I rushed around the apartment. It was my intent to hide every trace of the portrait before Rachel arrived. She might think it was too much – which would be fair, because it was.

Almost everything had been hidden away by the time a knock sounded.

"Damnit."

My hand was on the front door's lock when I noticed it. The freezer door hung ajar, a paint palette awkwardly blocking it from closing. I would not allow any chance of her asking about the portrait. It wasn't ready yet. I wasn't ready yet.

"Just a moment! I need to put on pants!"

Another 'Damnit' ran through my mind as I realized how stupid of an excuse that was. Not only were the pants I currently wore covered in paint spots, there wasn't any time to put on a nicer pair.

I mentally consoled myself as I rearranged the freezer so it could properly shut.

Everything is okay. Everything is good. She won't notice, she might not even care.

These thoughts would've been easier to believe if they'd actually come from Polimony.

I pushed the guilty thought of her from my mind, and opened the door. "Sorry, it's been a really wacky Wednesday!"

The worry surrounding my clothes worsened. Rachel's legs went up into a tan skirt, which stopped somewhere beneath my sweater from last Sunday. She had done her hair as well, exchanging the usual flat texture for curls. The new style perfectly framed her face. She was a living portrait free of any cover ups. She'd been smiling for a while, looking at me as I studied her in stunned amazement. When our eyes met I forgot everything else. That 'at home' feeling returned, loosening any anxieties I could've had before.

Warmth had found its way into my cheeks. "Hey," I gestured for her to come in, "sorry my place is kind of pathetic, I try to spend a lot of time outside of it."

Rachel laughed, kindly dismissing the hint of shame in my voice. "It's fine, I love it! It's really cozy..."

Something bumped into my leg as she walked in. I hadn't noticed, but she was carrying a picnic basket.

Before I could ask her about it, she'd already set it on the table and began walking around the kitchen.

"How do you afford a condo downtown?"

I awkwardly rushed between her and the fridge. "Haha, I told you, I paint for a living. And, it's only an apartment; a rental."

"I thought you were being funny!" Rachel turned around, her eyes darting between the sparse bits of furniture in the dining area. "*This,*" she gestured around for dramatic effect, "Is a condo downtown. You must be really good! What kind of things does this artist paint? Do you paint for other people or is it whatever you want?"

The fridge let out a decaying creek as I leaned against it. "A bit of both. Sometimes people commission me to paint what they want. Other times, I work on an idea and sell it."

As I spoke, Rachel began looking at the bare walls and clean floors.

She suddenly spun back to face me, "How come a painter doesn't have *any* art on his walls?"

I tried to think of an answer, looking the walls up and down for the first time in months. I didn't have many guests over, and so I had never been asked that before. It was a reasonable question. The truth was that there used to be a lot of pieces on display. But I didn't want to explain that. I didn't want to remember why there weren't any left. I wasn't sure that I could.

Instead, I just lied. "Believe it or not, the act of hanging wall art drives me insane. It's never quite right and, when it does finally end up on the wall, I start thinking of another picture to take it's place. It's easier to just avoid the process altogether"

Rachel smiled, narrowing her eyes. "You know, overseas they just lean them against the wall. I think you'd love it. The hassle of hanging, gone like that," She snapped her fingers for effect, "Stacks of paintings on the floor, picture it here."

Even though she was obviously teasing, it still hurt to imagine.

She giggled, seeing the pained look on my face. "Sorry, I had to. They really do that though, just not stacks. It looks a lot cleaner than what I described. You might really like how it looks."

I pointed at the picnic basket, changing the subject. "I've got to ask, what's in the basket? Is that the surprise?"

Her cheeks reddened, "Oh, yeah, do you like picnics?" She beckoned me over and opened it, "I don't really know what people make for picnics. Cheese sounded right, but you can't have cheese without wine. And then of course there had to be crackers too. None of it is cold though, because of the delay on the monorail. Oh, but there are a couple sandwiches. They should be okay. Should I put it all in the fridge or freezer for a bit? I don't mind if any of it is warm. And, I think wine is supposed to be better warm... Simon?"

My heart raced as the inside of the fridge came to mind.

"No, I love warm food! Humans haven't had refrigeration for most of history. Sort of makes cold temperatures an acquired taste, doesn't it? Good thing I haven't acquired it!"

Rachel beamed, "I love that! Hey, so I have everything in the basket that we need. I even have a little sheet like in movies."

"Like a bed-sheet?"

"No goofy, a thick one. We're putting it on the ground after all."

"Oh, sort of like a comforter?"

Another soft giggle escaped her, "Yeah, like a comforter. Except the uncomfortable kind that an old relative would use in their guest room."

"That actually sounds very cozy right now. Let me put on some new pants, I'll only be a minute."

"Didn't you just change?"

My chest tightened, "Ah, yes, but I was in such a hurry to see you that I hadn't checked these before putting them on. You look so wonderful, I can't help but feel a bit ashamed of my appearance. Especially if we will be going 'out' out."

"Ah! See that's the thing, I had a really fun picnic planned out! But, in my imagination we were in a forest on a hill."

I tried not to laugh, "A forest?"

"Don't make fun of me! The forest would've been perfect."

I ended up laughing anyway, "*The forest~*"

"Well, wouldn't you agree!?"

"I know, I know, it's just the way you describe wilderness is really funny to me."

"Okay, then where does an urbanite, like yourself, host a picnic?"

"The roof I suppose. Have you ever tried that?"

"For most of my existence roofs have been off limits. I have never even been on the roof of my own apartment complex, let alone any other tall building."

"How long have you lived here again?"

"That isn't fair! If everyone here falls off their roof I'm supposed to follow?"

I smiled and reached for her hand. "Come on. You are missing out on something right above you."

The clang of common shoes on steel steps rang throughout the narrow roof access. In this building, the stairs to the roof were opposite the elevator on the top floor. The stairs themselves were behind a heavy door. The steps leading up were confined to a narrow chute, perhaps half the area of the elevator.

Despite the difficult access, the roof was covered in amenities left unchecked and unsoiled by local ordinance. The property manager didn't seem to care, and there was an unspoken rule among tenants that there were to be no additions visible from the ground. I couldn't recall if there was a spot specifically for picnicking, but I wasn't concerned. All we needed was a relatively flat space to consume warm cheese and wine on. Atop the dimly lit roof were a handful of short awnings, a small garden, and various pockets of secluded AstroTurf. To me, a small patch of fake grass on a bed of concrete wasn't exciting no matter how high up it was. But, with the look in Rachel's eyes, her forest might as well have been secluded here all along. As we made our way between planters and cheap patio furniture, the lack of anyone up here became pleasantly noticeable. It was quiet, wonderfully so. The height had muffled most of the troubling sounds of the city, and what was left was the dull tone of the world itself. As we made our way towards the edge of the roof, a few evenly spaced patches of AstroTurf became visible. One was immediately against the guard, a thick transparent barrier that kept us from falling to our certain end. Rachel beamed with wild amusement, digging in her basket for the sheet before quickly setting up our spot. The sun had set almost entirely, but there was still some light leakage baking the sky from behind the horizon. Watching her admire everything, I took notice of her figure in front of the hazy orange atmosphere behind her. For a split second, I just enjoyed the view of her without thinking of anything else.

Only for a split second. It took perhaps two for the insecurity to displace ease. "I'm really sorry about what I'm wearing, you look absolutely perfect."

She blushed again, as she awkwardly stabilized two glasses on our blanket. "I think you look perfect too, Simon."

Before I could say anything to ruin the moment, she fell backward onto her palms and patted a spot beside her. She remained fixated on the skyline through the barrier as I filled both of our glasses with wine. A passenger jet briefly broke the quiet as it soared upward through the few clouds left lingering in the sky.

Her mood suddenly shifted from elation to forlorn reflection, "You know I've never been in a plane before."

I sipped at the bitter sweet Merlot. For once, there was no tension to relieve. There was no warmth to feel that Rachel hadn't already brought with her presence. For once, there was just the tart taste and the cool glass.

I swished the dark liquid around, taking on her change of attitude, curious to see where it goes. "Weren't you overseas? In a place with terrible interior design?"

"I read that in a magazine. I moved here several months ago but, unfortunately, I am entirely domestic."

"How'd you get here then? Where'd you come from?"

The mystery of this woman seemed to only increase as I got to know her.

Rachel lifted her glass and shifted her gaze from the bright lights below to the now dim light above. "I drove. I drove a beat up station wagon from nowhere to somewhere. That must've been years ago."

"Where's nowhere?"

"I used to call it home, back when I thought I knew what a home was."

"What made you leave?"

"I didn't like seeing the same people everyday. Have you ever lived in a town Simon? Or even a small city?"

"Never for long."

"And why is that? It's because of everybody else. You would think that disliking everybody else would naturally bring you to a place with less people. As if less people immediately means less trouble for the closeted misanthrope. Small towns are for the people-obsessed. This city is paradoxically *crowded* with antisocial folk - and I love it!"

I nodded my head in silent agreement, knowing all too well what she meant.

"I couldn't stand home. I didn't even have a frame of reference for a place like this, yet I still knew that I had to go. And this was before my clairvoyance! I can't imagine having to hear every single one of their thoughts... At the time, I wasn't confident that a place like this would be better. But I knew it would be different. That was all I needed, was somewhere *different*. Somewhere *else*."

She chugged her entire glass of wine and began pouring herself another before continuing.

"... Everything that wasn't essential was sold. Half of everything left ended up getting sold too. I had been saving up for a year, so there was enough to last until something was figured out. A quarter of my savings and a dozen headaches later, I finally made it... To the city beside this one. Between *there* and *here* isn't all that interesting. Mostly rising rent and juggled jobs."

Rachel began to sip at her second glass. Her eyes met mine, silently pleading for a verbal rest.

I put my glass down. "All of this travel... All the people I am sure you've met... And you've never been on a roof before?"

There was a slight spurt followed by a giggle as she choked on her wine. "No, never. This is a first!"

I chuckled as she seemed to return to her usual silly self. "Is it what you've always dreamt it would be?"

She laughed again, setting her glass beside mine. "No, not at all. I never imagined it in detail. Actually, I'd never imagined it at all. Roofs were always so boring in my mind! But enough of that, I think I have been talking about myself for too long. What did you do before you came here? Where are you from? Where is Polimony from? If you don't mind me asking."

I reached for my glass and drained it, holding up a finger as I hurriedly filled another and finished it in succession.

Rachel laughed, "I'm serious! Tell me your life story. Now. Go."

I rubbed the outside of my mouth against the inside of my shirt, a last ditch attempt at putting off the inevitable answers to her questions. "Well... Before *here* I'm not quite sure. We've been in this city for as long as I can remember... I don't know. It might just be blocked out or something. Things haven't been so great until very recently,"

I gave Rachel a warm look, "I don't want to bog you down with baggage though. It was a handful of bad relationships and I haven't dated in a while. Trying to recall the bad periods of my life is like trying to physically reach inside of myself: It might actually kill me. I know I've been painting my entire life. Portraits for as long as I can remember. Polimony has been around for just as long. Despite the bullshit, if it weren't for her I don't think I'd still paint. If I didn't paint I don't know what I'd do. She's always been this omnipresent muse of mine."

My heart sank a little with the recollection of the last interaction we'd had. "I wish I could tell you more."

Rachel moved her lips to the side of her face and thought for a moment. "Do you think *she* would remember your past?"

"If she can, she's keeping it to herself. I've been poking and prodding there for a long time."

Rachel paused again before smiling and reaching into the basket. "That can wait anyways, I only made a couple of sandwiches. Do you like warm cheese?"

"That depends, what kind of warm cheese?"

She smiled, apparently relieved to have stumbled us both past the heavy subject. "It's very orange and was bought at a discount."

I reached for the wine, and topped off both of our glasses.

XI

In between periods of consciousness, there is a lack of consciousness. This is the general assumption for anyone who doesn't investigate. I always assumed the same: that when I went to sleep or slipped away for a moment, I was gone and nothing had taken my place. This isn't true. Not for anybody. Certainly not for me.

...

A sharp shock bolted down my spine causing my eyelids to pull apart. The separation was slow and came with an uncomfortable peeling; a night's worth of crust had accumulated. Things slowly came into focus as I rubbed away the excess gunk. The artificial light of the city night illuminated the gaps between a set of blinds, creating a ghastly monochromatic outline of a large window. It was my window. This was my bedroom. Things continued to sharpen, and as more dim outlines sprung from the darkness into view, I could feel the bed move. Specifically the rise and fall of the space beside me, and the presence of limbs lazily pinning me in place. A stale smell slowly made note of itself while my entire view of the room began to shake gently with each throb of my head. When I tried to remember, there was nothing. It wasn't the usual fog or total black out. I began to panic in place as a tingle traveled down my spine.

You're so dramatic.

I looked towards Rachel. She was still, entirely, asleep.

Stop being such a Worry-Wendy. She's in bed with you, what are you so concerned about? Everything will be fine.

It wasn't her voice anyways.

Everything will be fine....

The words rattled around my head, the implications following shortly thereafter. Everything would be fine.

I spoke aloud, not necessarily to myself, "Everything is fine."

Yes.

But something wasn't fine. Looking again at Rachel, any fear of waking her up began to dissipate. She was sound asleep. Enough, almost, to make me worry. I would have called the police if it weren't for her slow but steady breathing. Or, perhaps, I would have called a lawyer. At the very least, I would have been very concerned. I gently lifted each of her stray bits off of me; making sure to move them as little as possible.

There was no need to turn the lights on in the kitchen, I knew exactly what I needed and where it was. My hand awkwardly fumbled for my favorite cabinet door.

"Oh?"

My hand bumped into it as I reached for it. The door was already open. Odd, but it didn't matter - so long as the contents were still there.

"Hmm..."

My hand bumped into nothing as I reached for a bottle. The cabinet was empty. This was unacceptable. The last thing I reached for was the light switch. To my great relief, it was still there. Details in both the kitchen and dining room became brightly lit. It wasn't difficult to piece together what had happened. Through the evidence left behind, it was obvious that it had been an interesting night. What remained of my liquor cabinet was unevenly distributed across the table. An open picnic basket was thrown onto the counter. There were empty glasses, plates of old cheese, scribbled notes that seemed to denote nothing at all. Newspaper clippings and photos were strewn all over the place. It was by complete chance, scanning the room for more clues, that I happened to see the answering machine was off. Naturally, I went on to check whether the machine was plugged in or not. It was.

On top of everything else, that was infuriating.

Why does that thing bother you so much?

All things considered, Polimony might have been right. There wasn't any real reason to be so angry. There was no evidence of anything to be mad about. And yet, for some reason, I still was.

I told you. Everything is fine.

"You said 'everything *will* be fine.'" I looked around again, amazed at what I had so clearly missed.

"I can't believe I've forgotten such a good time."

Polimony walked out in front of me, apparently coming from somewhere behind me.

At least you didn't forget a bad time.

"That is true...."

Inspecting the bottles left out, a small portion of two were more opaque towards the bottom.

"Bingo."

The contents of one was emptied into my stomach, while the other was left for later. Given what remained, it was hard to imagine Rachel helped to consume even a third of what was missing.

"I would have never taken Rachel for a drinker."

Polimony stared at the mess, contemplating something.

Me neither.

That was the next phrase to circle about my mind as I slunk back towards the bedroom. As soon as my feet were adjacent to that little slit under the door, a light began on the other side. When I opened the door there was Rachel. She was fully clothed and seemed to be looking around for something, until she saw me. Then she froze. Rachel tensed as I came near her, her body stiffening with my touch.

I drew away, unsure of what to do. "Is, something wrong?"

She shook her head like there was literally something knocking around inside of it. "No, you just startled me. That's all."

I tried to make eye contact with her, but she kept looking away. "If it was something I did, I'm sorry but, I don't recall."

Her entire body seemed to tense and relax as I reached for her face. As I draped the back of my fingers against her cheek, our eyes finally met

"Simon... I have to go. I left a note in a place only you will find it. It is only for you. Make sure you are sober when you find it so you can be alone. Do you understand?"

I followed her to the front door.

As she opened it and began to leave, she paused for a moment. "Simon?"

I couldn't help what came next, "Was it something I did? I'm sorry. But I don't know unle–"

"–Simon I really like you! I thought I told you that earlier? *You* did not do anything wrong. *You* should figure out some way to be alone; with that note and or with me. Now when is your big art auction? I have to go, but we need to talk before then. It's really important that only you and I talk, I cannot stress that enough."

"... The auction? I don't know. I've been really busy, and cooped up, and it won't matter anyways if I don't finish the – Hey, how do you know I'm in the auction?" I snapped my fingers, "That's it isn't it, I drank too much and gave you an ear beating. A painting is definitely a lot, one might even say excessive, I disa–"

"Simon! Why would I give you grief for painting me? And why would I give you grief for drinking? I drank more than you! Did you forget?"

My eyesight bounced between Rachel and the hallway carpet. I did forget, but I didn't say anything. I just looked at the carpet.

"You did forget. But only you did. Simon, I've never seen you get drunk. I still haven't. You've been drunk before though, and you've blacked out I'm sure."

I said nothing as she continued.

"And so you would know that people usually remember themselves drunk before things begin to blackout."

The carpet's pattern was geometric. The triangular outlines made me feel better for some reason.

Rachel shook her head. When I glanced up at her she was leaned against the wall, staring at the same carpet. Everything kept feeling off and I had no idea why.

"Simon? I'm sorry. I didn't mean to be so blunt. There is a chance that I'm only mad at myself. I don't know what to do about it, and I don't know what you're going to do either."

"About what?"

Rachel sucked in a lungful of air.

Then, she looked deep into my eyes, perhaps into my soul, and lightly held my face in her hands. She released her breath in a burst of whispers that seemed to slice the air around us. "Stop drinking and then find the note. Then call me. Alone. And Simon, listen to this, are you listening?"

I bobbed my head, still unsure of what to do.

"Don't touch that portrait. Sell it unfinished if you have to, it'll make sense soon enough."

She concluded her instructions with a quick peck, and an animated sigh. With that, she turned around and left. When I closed the door I almost jumped. Polimony was on the other side of it, awkwardly positioned against the wall.

Her.

I narrowed my eyes, "What the fuck, dude?"

Why are you staring at me like that?

"Why is Rachel acting like that?"

Because she's crazy. I don't know how you are surprised right now.

"I am surprised because you said last night was fine. As if you knew. And now she's acting skiddish and weird. It leads to a lot of questions."

And they have so many answers!

My muse awkwardly stumbled as she tried to follow me into the kitchen.

"Yes! Apparently hidden! In a location I'm supposed to magically know! Oh, and get this, on top of me supposedly knowing things that I don't actually know, I am meant to hide these things from you! Someone I share all of my thoughts and perceptions with! She's lost her mind, clearly. But nobody just loses their mind; somebody's got to knock it out of their hands or take it from them."

She couldn't have simply misplaced it?

I shook my head, recalled where the rest of the booze was, then shut the liquor cabinet. Polimony remained fixed to the center of the kitchen as I paced around her. I would change directions here and there, endlessly recalling something only to forget moments later.

You know Simon, time doesn't freeze when you walk around. Simon? Stop it. Stop.

"No, no no no, this is different, things feel different and I have no idea why. This is only another outward manifestation of what's been wrong."

Time doesn't stop when you overthink things either.

There was a ripe slap as I planted my bare feet on the flat tiles. "What should I do then?"

Polimony stared at me for a moment, and then at the floor.

Nothing. You don't have to do anything at all. I only wish you'd stop treating me like I'm the reason that things don't make sense. I'm not.

And, with that final statement, I was alone. I could even feel it: the lack of her presence. Alarmingly, feeling this only brought to mind all the times I was supposed to feel this and didn't. I shook away the intrusive thoughts, instead steadying my mind on the object of Rachel's note. "A place only *I* can find it?"

XII

For quite some time now, I've observed other lives lived in wretched routine. I always thought that it was a consequence of reason. I always thought that perhaps if one were to live without reason then there would be no predictable pattern to their experience; it would never be bland - That true chaos would be some sort of escape from the prison of order that most everyone else is subject to.

I was wrong.

...

The sensation of Polimony's absence was all that remained of the past few hours. My home was a mess, but still there was no note. Kitchen tiles teased at my tailbone until finally I stood and seized at the air with white knuckles; the real loss finally presenting itself.

"WHAT HAPPENED!"

The bedroom had been flipped, reset, then flipped again. There were art supplies scattered about the dining/living area, and everything smelt like garbage – because of course if the note weren't taped beneath the table, that only leaves the warm refrigerator. Looking around at the hopelessness, it was hard to stay angry. The emotional vacuum it left behind was enough to suck away any joy the situation could have brought. Left alone, was the loss itself.

"Where is it?"

Stray light bounced off of an empty bottle and into my eye from across the room. I gave my fingers a sharp snap, the bright reflection might as well have been an iconic light bulb, fixed in place above my head. Immediately, I ran over to the phone. There was a moments pause, and then a dial tone, as I steadied the receiver in the nook of my neck.

The other end rang twice before a voice chirped through the noise. "Aha! The call I have been waiting for! How goes it my friend?"

Finally someone that doesn't trouble me. My own soft breath tapped the receiver as I slowly returned to reality and away from the situation at hand.

"Mark, You have no idea how happy I am to hear your voice."

There was a quiet on the line, and then a rumble of a laugh. "Of course you are happy my friend, a new piece! A new piece of a new piece! What more could either of us ask for?"

I threw up in my mouth a little, trying to mask the odd upset with a cough. "Sanity, Grounding, I scared off my new piece."

"Slow down *Simone*, what new piece?"

"AH!"

There was a short pause on Marcus' end after I briefly screamed into the receiver, "Okay, okay... Come to the shop. It is a slow day today and you sound like you need to get out of there."

I scanned the room, still surprised to find a lack of Polimony. "Give me a couple hours. I need to finish something up at home."

"Anytime buddy."

There was an abrupt scratch as Marcus hung up on me.

"Dang it."

I put down the receiver, and surveyed the absolute mess I'd made. Maybe Rachel was crazy. Or maybe it was me. Someone had to be crazy, otherwise it wouldn't look like I was just robbed by a hoard of very picky thieves. In all the madness that had come to pass, a few warm cans of beer along with a half a handle of gin were discovered. Peaking at the small stash conjured Rachel's final instructions to mind,

stay sober... it'll make sense soon enough...

She was right. But still, maybe she was crazy. Or maybe I was crazy because she was right. Smiling, I relished in the satisfying snap of a fresh beer. Then, I quickly set the can down after tasting it. It was not good warm. Of course, there was tradition as well. Reaching for the bottle, I saw a strange reflection in the side of the leftover can. A tall, stretched view of my torso. It would have escaped me, were it not for the same reflection appearing as I set the bottle down. Momentarily, I considered the possibility that I'd gotten a tattoo. Unlikely in any state. Quickly, I finished the bottle and lifted my shirt. Then what Rachel said made sense.

ACT III

XIII

There has never been a time in my life where I could fully exhale. To be more specific, there has never been a time when I could fully be breathless and not worry about the next breath. Unable to be at ease, I always kept a small amount of wind in me. Sometimes, life knocks that out of you. But, when you are unable to part with it, the empty feeling lingers and becomes something new. In a way, I've still never been able to fully relax. That's why I wasn't able to be alone anymore. I didn't want to suffocate without anybody around.

...

"Polimony?"

Are you okay?

I was on the floor, dazed and with the feeling that I was weightless. Polimony sat at the kitchen table looking down at me. She appeared sullen, though it wasn't pity or shame. It was something else.

"Yeah, I think I passed out. I should probably make a glass of water."

In an instant, there was a glass of water on the kitchen table. As I stood to meet it, it wavered a bit. The shimmering glass seemed a mirage, though the cool liquid met my dry lips just as any other water would.

"That's convenient... Should I go to a hospital? That doesn't usually happen."

You're fine. It's just a side effect of your current condition.

"Hence the sudden urge to seek medical care. What is my current condition? A stroke?"

I looked down at my crotch and was met with bare flesh. "Where is the note?"

Simon...

Looking at Polimony's thighs, marked letters trailed upward and underneath a skirt.

"You. You have it. You are, how?"

We should go to the park! I think there are lots of leaves there, and I can get some fresh air while I explain that.

"Leaves? I'm not a child, and if anyone needs fresh air right now, it's me."

All the more a reason to go outside with me!

"You're ridiculous, I'll humor this but I won't be led on."

Polimony chuckled nervously, snorting a little in the process.

The park was unusually slow. At this time of day there should have been a lot more bodies present, people going this way and that, transient traffic making its way from point A to B; from home to work and perhaps visa versa. The ground was coated in a sparse layer of dark and decaying plant matter. Atop the dead the leaves, incandescent shades of orange and yellow were cast. The same shades illuminated bold faces of buildings around us, spires of illuminated brick and steel jutting forward from gray concrete and glass. Polimony soon led me to a bench near a fountain. Everything was situated in a way so perfect, it could've been a work of art all its own.

I sat at the bench while Polimony crouched by the fountain. The old wooden slats beneath me remained rigid, a reminder of my new weightless state.

"What is this about? Am I dying? Is this some form of advanced alcohol poisoning?"

It's been a very long time since I've been outside and felt the sunlight like this.

"We go outside all the time."

I mean actually being here

It was becoming easier to lose patience. A tremble began to move through me, and it seemed to move through Polimony as well.

For a brief moment, I was on the bench alone, and then once again I wasn't.

You haven't had that much to drink. You aren't dead, though arguably you haven't been alive in quite some time.

I clutched my abdomen, though not from any kind of sickness of abstinence. "What would that make you then?"

Polimony teased the water with her fingertips – with my fingertips.

Do you remember the last time you asked me that?

"No, but the answer would be the same then, wouldn't it?"

Yes.

There was a silence as Polimony stared at the fountain, still playing with the water.

More decaying bits of brown and orange floated around us, a gentle breeze had knocked them from the dry limbs above.

"Hello?"

Hi

"Is this about before? I never said we were done for, just that I want more."

Polimony stood up but still didn't face me.

Had you ever once considered what I wanted?

"I figure we can share her, like a schedule sort of thing. Maybe she'd be into that."

I don't want Rachel, I've never wanted any of them.

The park was so quiet. All that could be heard was the breeze, the occasional foot step, and the rustling of leaves against one another as they tumbled about. I realized then that I couldn't hear Polimony either.

"Polimony?"

What do you really want Simon?

I couldn't hear her at all.

A slight pain began to permeate the core of my head. The pain radiated outward, stinging the inside of my skull. I reached for my flask and, to my surprise, I found it.

"I suppose all I ever wanted was you..."

Polimony finally turned around. She looked the same as she always had, but she wavered slightly. I looked at the flask in my hand and shook it a bit. The container was half full.

"... And despite this cartoonish and annoyingly dramatic display, that's still at least one of the things I want."

Simon, what do you mean?

"Are you kidding me right now?"

She began to shimmer as my hands began to shake. Not from some kind of withdrawal or protracted hangover, from the emotions that the situation had stirred within me. It was frustrating, it was nerve wracking, it was –

CLINK Clunk CLUNK.

The flask had fallen from my hands, its contents slowly spilling on the ground in front of me. Polimony gasped, more taken aback by the mistake than me.

"That would concern you, wouldn't it."

My muse began to shimmer more.

"You can stop doing that, I can take a hint.

What ever do you mean?

"Just be quiet while I fish some of this up."

Her form became solid again as I bent over to pick up the flask. Perhaps now only a quarter full, the gin had comfortably settled into a relatively concentrated puddle. Stooping to my knees, I licked at the pool of ease and comfort. Somehow, an aftertaste of stagnant dirt had managed to penetrate the usually sterile burn of the alcohol. I washed away the germs with the remainder of the flask.

"Before you annoy me about germs, keep in mind that the alcohol sterilizes."

I doubt anything you get from the ground will compare to the sickness of going without.

Polimony was above me. The writing on her thigh was gone. I took mental note of this and stowed the thought away for the time being.

Something odd was happening but I something stranger prevented me from dwelling on it.

"... You'd be surprised what people leave behind in a public park."

I stood up, the awkward tension of nerve and discontent replaced by the familiar warmth.

It's really that simple.

"An easy fix for a complicated problem. But you knew that already, hence all of this."

I was going to tell you, that's why –

I cut her off, "I'm going to see Marcus. I can't believe you drained my stash to prove a point."

... There was some left behind.

"There was *enough* left behind."

When the MTA bus stopped at the 4th Avenue shopping district, Polimony and I waited for a few seconds. As the initial trickle of awkwardly sized passengers rushed off to be financially taken advantage of, a pocket of space opened up. We were able to comfortable leave the bus. Little droplets of water speckled and spattered the concrete around us. A moist monochromatic polkedot pattern formed on the sidewalk, slowly being consumed by the thickening rain. In spite of it, we made our way through the ebbing curtains of moisture to our final destination: Marcus' Paint Shop. Specifically, the basement. Unfortunately, the door was locked and the lights were off inside.

That's unusual.

"It's a sign."

A sign? The sign says closed. What do we do now?

"We go to a bar, we're in the First Ward, and we're on 4th Avenue. There are probably multiple bars on this street."

They don't sell bottles do they?

"Of course they do. But this time I'm going to be buying the bottle one shot at a time, poured into a little glass."

You're an ass

"And I'm becoming uncomfortably sober."

I limbered up the sidewalk, making little thought of the pedestrians that bibbed and bobbed about. "Plus, shouldn't we treat ourselves? We've done something excellent after all."

I'm glad you're finally saying 'we.'

I raised my shoulders and squirmed through a set of chairs and tables set out in the walkway. We met a gap in the greater obstruction of cluttered sidewalk furniture, it punctuated the outside of what appeared to be a business that sold alcohol.

"Well, here we go!"

A gaunt waiter greeted us before we could make our way inside, "Hello, would you like to hear our house special today?"

"No no no, I want vodka. I want vodka inside of me. Three shots of vodka inside of me."

"Ah yes, follow me."

I trailed the slender fellow, Polimony in tow behind me. "... And could you make it neat? No ice I mean, I don't want any cold little obstacles in my drink!" I chuckled at my own joke.

The waiter let out a slight grunt and led us to a booth by a window. "Vodka? Give me a minute."

Polimony sat in front of me, eyeing the place from every conceivable angle. The inside of the bar was completely covered in green felt. It wasn't cheap felt either. It was bright and well made, the type of texture that demanded to be touched. Everything was soft. It explained the sign behind the counter that said 'Soft Spot.'

True to his word, within sixty seconds our waiter returned with a tall glass of clear liquid.

I sniffed the drink, "What kind is this?"

The waiter smiled with his eyes half shut, "It is the house brand, Silk. Smooth like silk too. Perhaps even... *soft* like silk..."

I cringed slightly, immediately trying to ignore what he had just said. "What's the secret?"

"I can tell you, in exchange for fifteen dollars."

That's ridiculous.

I crossed my arms and sank into the pillowed felt of our booth. "Is that how much a drink costs?"

Our waiter stroked his chin and looked at the ceiling, "No. That is the tip you will give me in exchange for this information."

Extortion.

"Exciting!"

I fished a couple notes from my wallet and placed them on the table for the waiter to see.

The man swiped the money as I drained the glass in front of me. Almost no sting, soft like silk.

As I set the glass down, he cleared his throat. "Ahem, thank you sir. The secret?"

"Yes yes, what Is it?"

He brought his lips to my ear, and whispered low: "Water. And. Sugar."

"What?"

"You didn't hear that from me."

That makes sense.

"That's what soft liquor means? I don't want soft liquor, I'm trying to get drunk."

"Then buy more! They are so smooth!"

"I want to buy a few brand name bottles, I'm not sure if I like the house special."

The waiter went away, and before I could further think on the ordeal he returned. When he came back, he was wearing a hat and held two large bottles of clear liquid. They both appeared sealed at the top.

I scrunched my face as I observed them closely. "Couldn't you have just cut the vodka then sealed them? I don't see a label or anything."

The gaunt waiter tilted his head. "Do you not trust the house?"

"No. I don't. The drink you gave me didn't give me a buzz at all either."

Is this even a bar?

"That is because you only had one!"

"This is stupid. Just let me pay for the drink I had, I don't want a bottle."

"You're loss buddy, three shots is seven fifty."

I dug around in my pockets for some money, the contents being incorrectly rearranged as a consequence. Out came several coins and a lighter, the latter finding its way into the other pocket in a fit of split-second reorganizing. "Keep the tip."

The waiter grinned, "Very nice, very nice."

In the short time we were in there, the sun had risen and dried up some of the water from before. The street had taken to that 'just-rained' smell, it seemed to cling and linger on every single thing that crossed it. Luckily, only a block away was another bar. This one was more menacing. Black bricks and chains were fixed to the exterior. The overall theme looked like a cross between modern punk and retro goth; the medieval type. The overlap between the two had generated a very intimidating establishment. A chalkboard on the outside cheerily advertised that it was happy hour. The interior was lit in red and orange light. There were actual candles strewn about, each table having it's own, some lit some not. Distant clinking could be heard, it would seem that those who came here did there best to immerse themselves in the theme. Perhaps Simon and I could do the same. The actual bar was made of concrete blocks sealed in some sort of gloss.

A gloomy bartender tore a piece of paper and handed it to a few other patrons before shuffling towards us. His voice carried much more energy than his appearance, "Welcome to the Gauntlet. I'm Ryan... I read auras, and I see something interesting in you."

Polimony spun in her stool beside me.

Here we go.

I straightened up, "Is that so? What do you see?"

Are you really going to entertain this?

Ryan was quick to humor himself, "I see two distinct auras in you. I see one dark, and one bright. Tell me, do you carry any one with you? Any relatives or lost souls? Any travelers of any type?"

A nervous laugh squeezed its way through me and I instinctively reached for my flask. It was empty, of course. "I need a drink first, I think I might actually be dying now."

"That is definitely something I can help you with."

Ryan grabbed a glass, a bottle labeled 'Vodka,' a few other colorful containers, and a shaker, and began mixing them in one smooth motion. Within a few seconds a glass of swirling colors was presented before us. Ice somehow dusted in salt broke the surface of the solution.

Polimony peered wide eyed at the glittery, physics defying, surface.

Why can't you be the type of alcoholic who drinks drinks like that? Why does it always have to be this back alley shenanigans with you?

I shooed her away and drought the glass, gesturing Ryan over as the empty glass met the bar top. A wave of much needed relaxation came on immediately as we both readjusted ourselves in our seats.

THAT is 'soft like silk'

"No kidding,"

A bit of spit suddenly caught itself going down my windpipe, I choked a bit and grabbed the bar.

Ryan rushed over, "Hey man, is everything alright?"

"Yes," I cleared my throat a few times and pounded my chest, "everything is fine. In fact," It was a very stubborn bit of spit, "I could use another drink actually."

"Yeah I can do that for you, but are you sure? That was weird. What you just did there was weird."

"Heartburn, totally fine."

Ryan shut his eyes and shook his head, "Can't drink on an empty stomach. We have food here."

"No, not yet. Need a bit of padding for that."

"If you say so."

Polimony's eyes met mine as the bartender went to prolong our condition.

Do you ever worry about dying?

"No, and what is death to you anyways? Have you forgotten what we've talked about? There is a lot more that comes with this. In fact, it could be argued that you should put yourself in all kinds of dangerous situations, for the sake of either growing as a person or going to the next plane."

What? I was talking about your lame coughing fit. Is that really what you think?

"Essentially."

I promise you, there are better ways to live this life.

Polimony fidgeted a bit. Ryan seemed busy with a group of kids that had come in. I stood up and left a few notes on the bar top. I'd gotten all I needed from here.

The wind had picked up again as before, but it wasn't a cold wind. It was the the sort of soft breeze that would brush against you as you walked, gently cooling spots of heat left by the sun. 4th Avenue went on for a few more blocks, and I was eager to make the distance.

Weren't you going to buy a bottle for yourself?

"I'm not going to pay for a bar bottle I think there is a craft liquor store down here. Plus, Marcus' shop won't be closed all day. It's Friday, he's probably just taking a break or going to the bank again."

Oh. Well, what do we do until then?

"I'm not sure. We could just wait out in front of his shop and get drunk."

Or we could just wait out front and get a little buzzed?

"I'm already a little buzzed."

I'm glad you see our arrangement for what it is, but you don't need to be drunk. These actions take a toll on our body, and our soul.

"Our soul? Do you think we share a soul, or are there two souls in this body?"

I'm thinking about a lot of things, and none of them have anything to do with your existential ramblings. I don't want you to die from cirrhosis.

"I won't. I can get a new liver for us."

But then someone loses a liver.

"Car accidents happen."

You're being evil.

"They are accidents! There is no malevolence in an accident. Plus, isn't extracting a positive from something so negative quite good of me?"

Self motivated. Easily avoided.

"Easily solved. Fairly. And worst case, I'm sure Marcus knows someone who can get me a liver."

In a just world, that liver would come from someone who died from cirrhosis.

"Now you're the one being malevolent."

Polimony shrugged as we both stopped to enter the craft liquor store. A bell chimed as I pulled on the handle to Tammy's Craft Spirits. The inside was a kaleidoscope of colors. The floor was painted a rainbow spiral, each color bleeding up the walls and continuing along the ceiling. There was a color code in place, different drinks arranged in their respective hue.

Purple!

"Is there any white though? Or clear?"

A woman came pushed a cart of various bottles from behind an aisle. She wore red and black lingerie underneath a semi transparent dress.

Of course I noticed this, "Not leaving much to the imagination?"

The woman blushed, her name tag said 'Forgetful.' "It's part of the theme, I'm glad you like it, right?"

"Absolutely."

"If you're looking for clear liquors, they are along the Indigo stripe."

"Wait, these all look really nice. I don't suppose you keep the plastic bottles anywhere separate? I only need something to tie me over."

Forgetful nodded, "If you're looking for *that*, they'll all be mixed together by the beacon."

"Beacon?"

"Yeah, replace 'white' with 'bright' and then you've got it. You will definitely know when you see it."

No further questions could be asked, any I could've thought of were cut short by the quiet squeak of a cart wheel.

Forgetful was right. Near the back of the store was a white light that shone through the cracks of a couple aisles. There did seem to be a beacon of sorts in this liquor store. I crept towards the dramatic prop, Polimony lingered a few paces behind. The light was ridiculously bright, so bright in fact that the price tags around it were indecipherable. "Why? Why is it like this?"

The soft squeak returned and came to a stop as Forgetful chirped from a few aisles away, "The owner doesn't like people who don't buy the craft spirits. You're looking at the cheapest liquors in the store."

"I'm looking into a supernova, this might be illegal."

"You chose to go to it, I told you it was a beacon."

"You said bright! Not blinding!"

Her voice trailed off in a way so pronounced that she must have been doing it on purpose for a laugh, "Then close your eyes...!"

I palmed a few tall objects, cool plastic signaled that they were indeed the cheap stuff. Shielding my eyes, I made my way to the checkout counter where Forgetful had conveniently parked her cart.

"Find everything you need?"

"Yeah. I found everything I needed."

Polimony and I watched the bottles disappear into a black bag as the total added up to a satisfyingly low number.

That was illuminating.

XIV

I used to think that alcohol was this secret weapon that made me the person I was meant to be. It was as though every deep-seeded insecurity within me was intentionally placed so that I would one day find the key to unearthing them: some spare change and motivation. With something so simple I could be the person I wanted to be, the beautiful form beneath the scars. Liquor would peel back the layers of anxiety and leave what I assumed to be the authentic me. That person was someone else entirely.

...

I never really knew when Polimony slept. It felt reasonable to assume that she slept when I did, only occasionally escaping the window of my unconsciousness to annoy me or keep me awake. Despite evidence against this, I held onto this world rule as best as I could. Though in any case, when I was awake, she often was too. That was why when I suddenly awoke to feel an odd presence beside me, I knew it was her. The presence was odd, because it felt alert despite not moving. A person could simply intuit these kinds of things, in the same way they can tell a cozy home from a cluttered one despite the two looking very very similar. Then, there was a sound. It was a familiar melody that screamed in the ears in rhythmic thrums. Or maybe they were screeches.

I opened my eyes, the room tilted slightly and I realized I was a bit out of it. Sliced segments of city light scattered across my side of the bed. Polimony began to squirm and then push me, to no effect. The melody had fully become a screech, silent for a moment then repeating, louder and louder.

For G-d's sake can you turn that off!
"What?"
THE ALARM.

A tingle went through my body and the alarm was off and the bed was still again. When I peered beyond the bed, I couldn't see the time. Peering *over* the bed revealed a quiet alarm clock, laying face down on the floor.

"Polimony?"

She turned away from me.

"Polimony?"

I tried to shake her, but it wasn't worth much. I tried something harder for her to ignore.

AAAAAA! What're you doing!

She batted my hand away from her.

"Oh, so you can feel that?"

Yes. What do you think you're doing?

"I'm waking you up, the alarm was set for a reason."

Polimony flopped over and narrowed her dry eyes at me.

To bother me? To punish me? To make me miserable?

"All of the above. Get out of bed, I'm making breakfast."

I waited patiently at the kitchen table, half naked in only trousers and a button up. The cheap liquor from the day before was strangely more palatable when mixed with cold day old coffee. Marcus hadn't opened his shop and I had lost the motivation to wait. It was easier to just walk by it when I had what I wanted. I sipped at the tall glass beside me and almost gagged.

Polimony finally stumbled into the kitchen, a sort of tired excitement trailed behind her.

Where is breakfast?

"I don't know, it depends on where we go."

Polimony tilted her head at me and narrowed her eyes again. Pure contempt.

Really?

"Well I figured you could choose this time."

You actually woke me up just to make me miserable. I can't believe it, and yet in fact I can.

"No, I found the note Polimony, it's so stupid. You know that shit doesn't wash off."

What are you talking about?

I opened my legs and gestured to the slightly faded black ink trailing beneath my underwear.

Polimony briefly shifted her sight towards my inner thigh before jumping back to meet my eyes again.

I don't want breakfast anymore.

"You're so dramatic, and you were meant to ask me what it says."

I readjusted myself to appear more modest and tried to reread the short note. As I began to recite it out loud, a slow set of footsteps began to trail away from me and towards the bedroom.

Crazy. I told you. Absolutely insane. Thank you for waking me up for that.

I ran towards the bed before Polimony could reach it and stood between her and the warmth of rest. "Come on, that's funny! And to think we made such a big deal about it, now let me make us up some breakfast. It's clearly late in the morning anyways, why are you so eager to go to bed?"

Three reasons. One, you kept me up all night; and two, you didn't make breakfast. You never make breakfast.

"What do you mean? I always make breakfast."

No, you don't. You bitch and moan, and then buy some cheap fast food. Then you bitch and moan later when it makes you sick.

"That's why you're choosing the place this time!"

Simon, I'm gonna go to bed before I become more alert. There is still a chance that this ridiculous morning can evade my long term memory, like a bad dream.

There was a cold sensation as she simply went through me and rolled into the sheets.

Before reentering the kitchen I turned and regarded the breathing mass that had, perhaps intentionally, sprawled itself across the entire bed. "Wonderful."

I sat at the table and continued to work on my drink, peering down at the scrawled note after the odd sip and beaming with contentedness.

"She really is a work of art all herself." I mused.

The sudden urge to call Marcus was almost overwhelming, as was the simultaneous urge to check the machine for a message. I clicked the play button and was met with nothing besides the click itself. I prepared myself for the inevitable, and almost threw a fit when it came to pass. A dark, unlit LCD. Repeatedly plugging and unplugging the machine did nothing this time, the damned thing had finally given up the ghost.

"Landfill," the word crept from my lips and was soon replaced by another, "Auction."

Marcus's number was rapidly dialed into the reliable phone, and a I was able to breathe in relief when the other end began to ring.

The relief passed as soon as he picked up, "SIMON! Where the hell have you been? You're machine won't take my calls and neither will you,"

"I know, but –"

"No my friend, I KNOW. I know you are busy, I know you are sorry, but what you don't know is that the auction is in a week. You would have known that, if you had bothered to call or visit."

I flashed back to the breezy day on 4th avenue, walking by Marcus' closed shop twice. "I *tried* to visit yesterday, but you weren't at the shop."

Suddenly my old friend was much less aggressive sounding, "This does not matter. Forget what I said, all is forgiven. I need the portrait, are you home now?"

The portrait. The dust.

"I am, but it isn't quite right yet."

"It is never quite right with you! I want you to trust me Simon, it will sell. You will be happy with the price. And in return, you will paint something else. Maybe several something elses, but this is not important now. The gallery needs to have the painting in order to sell it."

"Marcus you don't get it. This is the final touch, the difference between mediocre and magnificent."

"I refuse to listen to you when you say these things, I will be at your home in an hour. Do not make me become a villain Simon! You know a good friend is capable of these things when they must be done."

He punctuated the dramatic threat by hanging up.

XV

It had been so long since I'd been home, so long since I'd been fully present for a morning sun rise, so long since I'd been myself. Sharing is a universal compromise that can often lead to contempt if done poorly. This contempt can precipitate into conflict, and then you don't share anymore. Growing up, I was an only child. This meant that I would have to become better acquainted with the concept of sharing later in life. In some ways, Polimony is like the other I never had. The annoying, judgmental, and possessive other that would teach me about sharing in adulthood. The trouble with our relationship is that, like me, nobody ever taught Polimony how to share.

...

Marcus said nothing after he buried his head into his hands. His entire body had somehow conformed to the shape of the chair at my kitchen table. There was half of a warm beer beside him. Aside from the slow deep breaths, it was almost hard to tell that he was there.

I continued to nurse at a glass of my own, desperate for any form of relief. "I don't know where it could have gone, it was right under the bed."

"What kind of artist keeps his work under his bed?"

"Where else would I put it?"

"The wall, this table, on an easel, in a great steel cage, or in my store. It would have been safe with me, you could have finished it there with all the supplies you may need all surrounding you. Why must you put me through these things?"

"Stop talking like it's been shredded and burned, it's only been misplaced. It couldn't have gone far."

Marcus exhaled and lifted his head. "How long did it take?"

"To paint the portrait?"

He nodded.

"About a week, but I can't just make another."

"Why not? You made the first one?"

"It isn't that simple, it wouldn't have the same energy."

"Energy? I do not need energy. I need something from you on that stage in seven days. I have made arrangements on on both of our names."

He stood up and began towards the door, "Tonight, I will bring you everything you may need for another."

"You still have a spare key?"

Marcus dug around in his pocket and began to shake what sounded like an unrealistic amount of keys, "It is somewhere."

I gave a half smile as he saw himself out.

Polimony appeared behind the door as Marcus shut it behind himself.

Well, this is quite a pickle you're in.

"Where the hell is it?"

How would I know?

"Surely you saw me put it somewhere, maybe last night."

I might've. But I was trying to sleep. Re-mem-ber.

"No, that's the problem. Do you think I could make another?"

Sure, but you might not have to. I'm sure it will turn up. Don't you think it's odd how he doesn't care about the quality of the end product though?

I began to pace between the dining area and kitchen, "He was exaggerating, obviously I can't just draw a stick figure expect him to be satisfied with that."

But, do you get the odd feeling that he might be?

"What does it matter anyways? *I* wouldn't be satisfied with that. Would you?"

Polimony sobered and said nothing.

"I need to find it but first I need to talk to Rachel."

My statement was met with a blank stare and a slow blink.

"Alone."

This again?

"She said she wanted to talk alone after I found her note. I've found it, and now I need to talk to her alone. That's fair isn't it?"

It isn't really fair to me though, is it?

"It isn't about fairness then, it's about boundaries. I want to spend a bit of time with her and, even if she's a bit silly, she seemed really serious last time I saw her."

I don't see why you keep doing this to yourself Simon.

"Doing what?"

Polimony gave me a look that was simultaneously empty and yet so full of emotion, it evaded description.

Hurting yourself.

"No, we talked about this already, there won't be any pieces this time."

She glanced away and seemed to think about that for a moment before looking back up at me.

Then why don't we make a game of it.

"I'm not sure I like how 'not-fun' that kind of game sounds."

It isn't fun. But it is fair. If things don't work out with Rachel, then no more.

"What? What are you on about? 'No more'?"

You know exactly what I mean. Every time you see some prospective infatuation, I warn you, you disagree, and then the same thing happens again. You know what the definition of insanity is right? So if the same thing happens with Rachel, then no more insanity.

"I don't see how you could ever enforce that outcome, but I'll agree on one condition."

Hmm. What would that be?

"You don't get to interfere with the two of us in any way."

Polimony faltered for a moment, apparently deep in thought again. Eventually she smiled much too cheerfully and reached out her hand.

I hesitantly shook it.

"You know, if you look up 'insanity' in the dictionary, you would see a different and more medical definition."

That doesn't matter! All that matters is how happy we're going to be!

"What?"

I'll see you later Mr. Alone Time.

And then she left.

I obviously knew better than that, but her dramatics weren't lost on me. Instead of dwelling on it though, I dialed Rachel's number into the phone and checked the machine. No red digits, no messages, no luck.

The other line rang a couple times before she picked up, "Simon!"

"Rachel, yes, are you home? I've got to see you. You come up everywhere I look, you know that?"

"Of course, but are you –"

"Great! I'll be there soon!"

I hung up and immediately got dressed. Finally someone who would be happy to see me, someone I was happy to see.

XVI

'Several' years is far from a long stretch in the grand scheme of things. Even at the ceiling of what the term could imply, it still isn't a dozen. The first time someone took 'several' years of my life, I remembered them. Several years later I still do.

...

I tried to keep my mind clear as I perceptually navigated to the nearest metro. It seemed that, for the time being, I was alone. Hopefully Rachel could help take advantage of that. Whether or not I could think about my current situation in private, I was not certain. Polimony's presence was gone, sure. But her lack of presence was no longer a tell-tale sign that she wasn't listening. Listening to very thought, and watching every interaction, in absolute silence. In this way she had done so much more than I had ever given her credit for. Though maybe right now she really was giving me the benefit of actual privacy. Or, maybe it didn't matter. Maybe –

A large suited man bumped into my shoulder, "Hey, watch where you're going, chump!"

I whipped around as the back of a navy blue fedora bobbed further and further away. "Chump?"

I had become so lost in my internal ramblings that I'd passed the monorail station by an entire block. A heavy wind blew down the street. A car honked in the distance. There were dead leaves scattered all throughout the road and sidewalk. It was as though the town itself was decaying beneath all of it. It was so easy to feel this way, each backtracked step a lost grain of sand in my hourglass of alone time. Granted, Polimony had never set a deadline. I was the one doing that. Before I could feel any worse about everything, I reached the steps of the station. There was an echo with each upward step, the sound of cheap shoes rhythmically tapping weathered steel. Eventually, I made it to the top. There was a single body besides mine in queue for the monorail. He wore a navy blue hat. His shoulders were such that they could have filled the entire station. The thick pads of his faded blue suit seemed to restrain them from doing just that. He stared at the empty tracks, frozen in place and apparently ignorant of my presence. A red tie seemed to stain a boringly white undershirt. There was something about him that seemed out of place. In fact, all of him seemed out of place. The wind picked up again, and no part of him was moved by it. His eyes remained fixated on the tracks as a monorail car slowly screeched to a stop in front of him. I stepped on, patting my pockets and quickly situating myself in one of the many empty seats. The doors shut, and the car began moving. Suddenly, I recalled the odd man. Nowhere to be found on the car, I looked through the windows. He had disappeared from the station as well. Slowly picking up speed, the car began to zip outward from the center of Warren. Nondescript towers of glass and steel came and went, slowly being replaced with decaying stacks of brick and mortar. Eventually, I began to see plywood framed window units. The brakes sounded and the rail car once again came to a stop. I only heard half of the standard transit announcement as I lunged for the stairway down. Deadline or not, I was on a mission. The route to Rachel's place was much more welcoming in the daylight. The sharp contrast brought to mind how little time we'd spent together. The tall apartment buildings seemed less intimidating and more generic. The graffiti blended into the various faded materials that they overlaid. Further away, the orphanage caught my attention. In the sun, it seemed so ordinary. But then again, it was, wasn't it? I dwelt on this, but only for a moment as I soon reached South forty-sixth Street. Rachel's street. I could already see the upper half of her building, the visible part slowly receding from sight as I reached it. There was an urgency that built within me as I entered, only to worsen as I waited for the elevator to arrive. The sounds of the building presented themselves fully in a way I had never noticed before. I could distinctly hear two separate television programs, both partially distorted by a phone call down the hall. A distant rattling sound from above seemed to grow louder and louder. The chaotic clamor was finally interrupted by a loud beep as the elevator arrived. Several elderly people filed out, leaving behind them a unique smell characteristic of their age group. I repeatedly pushed the button for floor seven, the doors lazily sliding shut in response. The smell seemed to intensify as the elevator cab began its ascent. The odd odor wasn't unpleasant, it just had the strange effect of making me want to leave. The elevator was quieter on the inside, but there was no music. The only sound besides dampened rattling was a monotonous chime that sounded as it passed each floor. My heart sped up with each beep until the elevator finally began to slow down and stop. I almost ran out before noticing a dimly lit "5" on the button panel. The lazy doors stumbled open, revealing, bit by bit, a petit blonde in what looked like mismatched wool apparel.

"Rachel?"

"Simon! Did you find the note? Are you alone?"

"I think so, and yes I found your note. Absolutely adorable by the way, Polimony didn't think it was very funny though"

Rachel shook her head and gestured for me to step out of the cab. "You *think* that you're alone? And you told *Polimony*!?"

"Can we discuss it at your place? It's only a couple floors up."

"No, it's on this floor."

There was a dull clunk as the elevator doors shut behind me. "I thought that you lived on seventh floor?"

"We are on the seventh floor."

An image of the dimly lit "5" briefly drifted into my mind before being displaced by something else. "I must be losing it."

She began to lead me away from the floor-lobby and towards , presumably, her apartment. "Well, I think I might know why. What do you mean adorable? Are we talking about the same note?"

I gestured towards my crotch for the second time in the same month, "Property of Rachel?"

Rachel blushed and shook her head as she fumbled for a particular key, "Then she might not know about the real note."

There was an oddly *clean* smell that tumbled out of the now open door of her apartment.

"What?"

The lock made a satisfying click as it was engaged.

Rachel had clearly deep cleaned and bleached everything. She brushed off the couch before she sat down, then brushing off the spot beside her and patting it for me. "Simon, I left you a voicemail. I figured you were the only one who actually checked that ancient thing."

"It isn't that old, I bought it new several years ago."

She chuckled as I as slumped beside her, "New to you maybe. Well, whether she's here or not won't matter I suppose. I'm sorry about the other day, and the other night. I had an amazing time on the roof *with you,*"

The last two words she said formed a rock that sunk into the bottom of my stomach.

"After we went inside, you changed. I thought it was odd that I couldn't sense Polimony's presence on the roof, but then your suddenly odd behavior that night wasn't odd anymore. They weren't odd because they weren't yours,"

The room began to warp and bend slightly as the rock in my gut grew in size and began to divide.

"They were hers. I'll admit, I wasn't that bothered at first, and by the time I'd actually put two and two together we were already in your room,"

The dividing rock formed a series of continuously growing and dividing stones inside of me.

"It wasn't until slightly after I jokingly wrote that note on your, or her, crotch. We were laying in bed, talking about you and your art. We talked about all your subjects and inspirations for your most popular portraits."

The endless torrent of gravel seemed to weigh me down more and more as Rachel began to speak in a more serious and cavernous tone.

"I started to talk about the photos, the arson, how it all connected and how worried I was about you. It was phishing of course. I was sure you'd been secretly well aware that every single one of your subjects has been burned alive."

The gravel turned to earth, to dirt, to mud, stretching the lining of my stomach and causing me to drip profusely from the pores.

"She just shut up. And I don't mean she was silent, she just walled herself away. But I could sense it Simon, the way she felt. In an instant she'd gone from swooning over you and your work, to a dark smolder. I couldn't tell if it was rage, but whatever it was, it was intense enough to make me question whether you even –"

I vomited all over Rachel's coffee table as the the rest of the room shifted into loose earth, burying me beneath it.

XVII

Keeping secrets wasn't in my nature. Maybe it was this that made it so easy to tell when I was doing just that. Such an inability to engage in deception made lying to anyone more trouble and effort than it was ever worth. This inclination towards honesty was enforced by the often slim chance of anyone on the outside finding out. I could only imagine how easy it was for Polimony to catch me in a lie from the inside.

...

"Simon, wake up!"

Rachel was standing in her own doorway, arms at her sides, eyes poised at me.

There was a deadening effect that an information dump had. But there wasn't any reason for me to be on the –

"Hello? I'm talking to you."

"For G-d's sake, I am trying to introspect!"

"I knew it, I knew you were back!"

Rachel ran directly towards me, crossing the gap in what seemed to be two strides. As she sank into me, I prayed that the couch would fall back or break – if only to bear at least part of the burden. Instead, I was made deeply aware of every bone in my body as I sustained her entire impact.

Rachel's arms wrapped around me as her muffled words fell into my shoulder, "I thought I had it figured out."

My arms found their way around her as my tone complimented hers, "I was really hoping you did."

She pulled away, the once security-seeking embrace rotting into something less, something confused.

"What do you mean?"

I cleared my throat, momentarily unable to speak, "I don't know what the problem is, but I know that there is one. I want to hold you for a moment. Don't look at me like that, is it so wrong to want you?"

Rachel loosened, and fell back into me.

"No. It isn't wrong for you to want me," again, her words found themselves trapped in my shoulder, "It's wrong for *her* to want *you*. It's wrong for *you* to want *her*."

For the longest time, I held her. And, for an equally long amount of time, she allowed herself to be held by me. There was a phrase to describe what Polimony did to me: It was though as she lived entirely at the tip of my tongue. Perpetually unknown and yet always present. Rachel felt like an answer, and yet the feeling still remained. The end result was a pull from both directions, something that I would need to get away from entirely if I were to ever reconcile the two.

"Rachel, what happened?"

Another stifled set of sentences warmed my chest, "She happened. I thought when you drank she took over, but now I'm not sure."

"Well, on the bright side at least I can drink. Plus, what use is my body if I'm hammered?"

She pulled away again, wearing an expression I'd never seen on her before. A mixture of confusion and disappointment blended in a single word, "What?"

I adjusted myself to account for the sudden lack of weight, "It was just a thought. But it sounds like she just comes and goes at times. You two got along before, I don't see why it's such a big deal. I know that it's weird, but maybe we can make it work."

"Simon, did you hear anything I just told you?"

"Well, to be fair, it was a lot all at once. I don't actually recall a lot of it. I do recall throwing up."

I attempted to gesture at the mess, but to my surprise it was gone.

She shook her head, "That is exactly my point. You aren't even aware that you lose time. And when she does take over, she isn't going for walks around the park. Do you remember any of what I told you?"

"Bits and pieces."

An index finger was slowly raised towards my lips, "She knows where the note is now, and she knows that I know what she is. If you know, I don't know what she will do,"

"You're saying 'know' a lot."

The side of her finger began to slightly press into my teeth.

"I love you Simon."

Suddenly her finger was lifted.

She shut her eyes and took a deep breath.

It was so easy to admire her as she leaned her head back, defeated by something I only had a vague recollection of. The almost cartoonish caricature of a woman I'd first met had come to morph into something else entirely. Something with a dimension beyond what any picture or painting could capture.

Or maybe I'd simply gotten to know her better.

"I love you too Rachel."

Her eye lids lazily opened, allowing her sight of the ceiling above her. I looked up, reminded of the blue sky above us. The blue sky she'd created for herself. "I've cleaned everything, I've packed all the things that matter to me. But I'll miss this the most."

"What do you mean?" I quickly looked around her apartment, "Everything's still here. Why would you pack? Are you leaving?"

The same lids lazily shut, "Even if you haven't finished my portrait, I'm sure auctioning it off is enough justification for her to set this all ablaze. I don't want to leave, but I don't want to be another one of your 'flames' that 'got away.' Neither of us wants that."

"But what about the Gentleman's Club? The Historical Society?"

"When you subtract all the arson that they are now exonerated of, it doesn't leave much. It hardly leaves a few."

Rachel opened her eyes again and looked directly into mine, "I love *you*. And because of that I have to go."

"Well, what if you loved *her* too?"

She pursed her lips, still keeping soft eye contact for the short time between silence and speech.

"Check your voicemail Simon."

She stood up and led me towards the door. When that failed, she nudged me. When nudging didn't work, she asked me to leave. With the door still open and with me in the threshold, I turned around. How could I not? The door to Rachel was literally about to close behind me. I wanted to say something, ask something, *do something*.

As if the signals could be too clear, she had to mix them up and share with me the greatest kiss I'd ever experienced. The kind of kiss that gives hope rather than takes it. The kind of farewell that couldn't have been final. And when her door closed behind me, I couldn't help but feel that this wasn't the end. In a way, it almost felt better than holding her. Almost.

ACT IV

XVIII

There is something deeply ingrained in me. An unending urge to be in the presence of another. More often than not, it remains unsatisfied. Perhaps that is what led me to Polimony. Or that may have been what led her to me.

...

With Rachel's door shut behind me, there was an unfamiliar silence that hung in the place of where the air should have been. The auditory vacuum was slowly replaced by a teasing electric hum from within the walls. Then, the ever distant sound of an indecipherable program on a television set, perhaps down the hall.

Still, I became more and more aware that there was nobody. Not even the touch-less presence of my muse. It was the imperceptible and yet all-encompassing sensation of true loneliness. It was a feeling I hadn't been acquainted with in a long time, and it was frightening. Despite this, each step down the now unfamiliar hallway of Rachel's complex was lighter than the last. Each breath I took unburdened by something I never knew was there. When taken with the kiss I'd just had it became a bitter sweet thing, and that is a rather exciting flavor to experience. The loneliness somehow felt like a means to an end, an ending that involved Rachel and I.

"It's not the end!"

My words were dampened by the elements of the hallway. It didn't dampen me though.

The worn carpet seemed fresh. The patched drywall and cracked ceiling rejuvenated. The broken elevator an exciting invitation to a now-new stairwell.

Heavy iron marred by decades of wear almost sprang open as the dull background of poverty was replaced by the monotonous rhythm of shoes falling on concrete steps. Faster and faster still, something better seemed to dangle in front of me at all times. This time tangible, this time real. In no time I had descended several floors. I burst forth into a warm lobby filled with stale cigarette smoke; the last antechamber between the past and present.

But I had to catch myself. I didn't want Polimony to be in the past. The lack of her presence wasn't what I really wanted. Even in my dreamiest fantasies of Rachel, Polimony was still there. Still my muse, still waiting for when it all fell apart. Even in my fantasies, everything falls apart.

There was nobody in the lobby besides me.

A sharp clang sounded as the heavy door to the stairwell shut behind me. Stray droplets crisscrossed the windows of the entrance to the building. It was raining, and it was dark. Standing there for what felt like a while, I pondered on the nature of what Polimony was to me. I loved her, and I did want her. Rachel was right about that. But if I were to ever truly love Rachel, I would have to shelf any feelings for another. That included Polimony. In that way, she became a sort of weight. She grounded me, but at the same time, she *grounded* me. Still, what was she to me?

Before I could make up my mind, a set of shallow footsteps clung to the space behind me, arriving quicker than possible. And I was no longer as alone as I was before.

Is that how you really feel about me?

"Polimony."

It was an excited whisper, and yet it came out with a touch of fright as I spun around to meet her.

Her quiet arms wrapped around me and her head fell into my chest.

Am I really such an awful burden for you to carry?

There was a deep hurt in her voice as she peered up at me.

"No... I love you."

Why aren't I enough then?

She already knew the answer. She already knew everything. And still, I lied.

Weakly, "You are enough."

Without disturbing a single atom of my physical being, her hold tightened. Perhaps directly on my soul.

I love you more than anyone could ever love anybody else. One day you'll love me too.

And before I could even pretend to object, she faded away. Leaving behind a bitter imprint.

"But, I do love you..."

There was no point in saying it. She had left of her own accord. The air in the lobby had stilled, as if waiting for what I might do next. As if I had a real choice.

The wind outside contrasted with the air inside so greatly that it was frightful. It whipped at everything, beating anyone brave or motivated enough to leave the many concrete and mortar shelters within sight. Even the trees seemed to loom lower than usual, their many decaying limbs grasping at the ground with terrifying tenacity. Gray skies hugged gray rooftops, buildings were bleakly outlined by scant moonlight.

A person needs some respite in trying times such as these. And so it was determined, unilaterally by me, to walk until something exciting happened. I spitefully stomped about the calamity. It was as though G-d Himself were just as determined as those around me, and to what end? I still wasn't sure. As I made my way down the street I had once committed to memory, the air began to thin and the walkways began to fill again. Not with water, but with people. They seemed friendlier than before, as though they were keen on the small triumph of a lonely painter. Within a few blocks, something exciting finally appeared. A rather retro marquee sign in the shape of an arrow.

Dimly lit bulbs hugged the marquee, they blinked on and off around an inviting question: "Te amo or Tequila?"

It was still sprinkling outside, but it had dried out considerably in a short time. The wind no longer howled but cooed. I could have summoned any excuse I liked, but I no longer needed one. A choice between my love or a stiff drink of latin origin was an easy choice to make, at least at present. Creeping over cracked concrete, I quickly found myself in front of the entrance. There was reflective chalk on the windows of the door, each of the many grid-arranged panes of glass was plastered in countless signatures. Some were worn, some quite new. Beside the door was a metal stool with a platter of chalk. Given the condition of the pieces that remained, I could only imagine how many had ever been stolen.

I resisted the urge to mark my arrival and headed in, the door of many marks swinging shut behind me. Inside, it was dark. There weren't many patrons at this hour, it had only recently become dark outside after all. However, in place of bustling business, there was an all-too-eager bartender waiting to empty my pockets in the most legal way possible in the area.

Cheap stick on tiles seemed to cushion each step as my back end met cheaper vinyl cushioning.

I briefly considered a non-alcoholic drink before the thought was cut off by a manipulative quip.

"You arrived just in time for happy hour!"

I shook my head in response, "That seems to keep happening to me."

The bartender nodded his head. A scrawny lad perhaps nineteen in age and certainly not older than twenty. A bright smile outshone what few facial features were visible in the mood-light of red LED's and incandescents. The different shades of either light source were keenly scattered by the irregular transparencies of glass filled with clear and opaque liquids. This was certainly a bar.

"That's a fifty cents a shot."

"Looks like you're getting a raise then. Give me two, dealer's choice – but don't act like it's *your* liquor."

It took a split second, as the boy turned around and bent over, for me to realize that I had just rightly earned a double shot of bottom shelf. As my glass was filled, it also became evident that I had earned slightly less than a double shot.

"I hope you enjoy that!"

"I meant to be funny, not mean."

"Oh, um, it was funny! Haha, see I am laughing!"

"That sounded fake, please give me better liquor. I'm sorry."

The bartender flipped between awkward uncertainty and self-amusement, "Only if I get to watch you drink that in one go."

I laughed, "You don't know who you're dealing with."

And within what seemed a moment, the glass was empty and I gagged on what can only be described as warm whiskey with the legs of cheap wine.

The bartender chuckled and refilled it, this time from a clear bottle within view.

"Good enough to not hide is good enough for you, sorry about that."

"Good G-d, where did you get that garbage?"

Suddenly, he appeared offended again.

"I've got a mind to give you more of it."

"What is wrong with the bars in this town?"

"I don't know, you keep choosing to live here."

"Whatever, close out my tab."

"You never opened one, that first one is on the house."

"Then how much will this one be?"

"I'm not sure yet."

I turned to to look away and met eyes with a stranger, a rather tall woman with muted features and pale skin. She looked disappointed with nothing in particular. My eyes darted to the right, quickly improvising and searching for anything else to grab my attention. There was nothing but much-too-shiny brown oak, tacky neon signs advertising no-name beer, and a pool table that appeared warped even from across the bar. I turned back towards the bartender, still the same lad.

"Bit of a dinky establishment."

"You're a bit of a dinky patron."

"What the hell?"

"I just work here."

"Have you decided on a price then?"

"Yeah, it's free if you leave."

I thought on that for a moment.

"Could I keep the glass?"

The pale woman to the side of me laughed.

The bartender didn't, "No."

I drained the glass as I had before, this time slightly less disgusted with its contents, and got up to leave.

"You're banned."

"What are you on about? I just got here."

There was a flash, followed by a mechanical whirring. The bartender had quickly taken my picture, placed the camera back in its discrete location, and was now dramatically fanning a fresh photo.

I dug a coin from my pocket, and threw it at him. The buzz from the poor liquor was already beginning to take hold.

There was almost no reaction from the bartender as he continued fanning the photo. "And now you're leaving, right?"

"Absolutely, this is ridiculous. You're a joke."

Quickly, I walked out. Dodging the odd floor board as I made my way to the exit.

As the old door swung shut behind me, there was the faint voice, "And stay out!"

In the short amount of time I was inside of that place, the outside had somehow become darker. Looking up, I was relieved to find that this was only because of a handful of new clouds obscuring the temporarily released moonlight from before. There was another storm coming, and in the face of such a setting my mind somehow wandered towards all that had occurred in the past month. My short encounter with Rachel, though far from over, had brought to the surface much of what I'd have rather left alone. Childhood memories always out of reach, fragments of the self that seemed to always stray from their origin. The focal point of everything evaded me with every attempt to conceive of it. As the fervor of liquor began to settle further, my feet began to wander beneath me, mindlessly dragging me towards a destination that I had to see. More concrete and more raindrops, humid air and dim streetlights. The odd human made space for what was most likely evident from first sight – a being on a journey. A traveler given flesh. I embarked subway and bus, a short path made complex by the intricacies of an urban landscape. Finally I arrived. There was the occasional boom of thunder, the even more infrequent flash of lightening, both given a backdrop by slow falling rain that silently came to surround me.

There is a feeling you get when retracing your steps, even I you didn't remember ever taking them. It was an absence of unfamiliarity in spite of itself. That was how I felt now, standing before tall slabs of rot metal. They were rusted throughout, and only in appearance did they guard the inside of the orphanage. It was immediately apparent that there was meant to be a lock of some sort, but there was none to be found. I hesitated then thought better of it, it would be even more foolish to leave after coming this far. With two hands, I pushed the doors inward. An unwelcoming screech punctuated my arrival into what could only be described as ruins.

The orphanage was in absolute decay. It was a wonder it hadn't been demolished in all the years it appeared to have sat and spoiled. A weed ridden courtyard spanned the space between the initial gate and the dilapidated structure within. The actual entrance to this place was nothing but a gap framed in brick, the doors having left the place long ago. I found myself lagging through this hole in the wall, still fighting off the odd second thought. Despite the initial nerve, there was nothing inside but more ruin. I flipped a switch by the 'entrance', surprised to see a row of tired incandescent lights dimly blink and flicker until steadily illuminating a surface of torn wallpaper. Broken furniture, apparently burnt, only added to the scattered evidence of a fire partially covered by what appeared to be thriving mold. As I stepped over seared floor boards, a creak reverberated around the room. A small bird flew from a pile and through one of many holes between the wall and the ceiling. Looking around, I felt foolish. There could be nothing left in a place like this.

Despite this apparent fact, there was the will that undermined it. My will, at least a will that seemed to come from within me. That same familiarity with that which is unfamiliar, it dragged me about in a sort of crude game of 'hot and cold.'

It pulled me in the directed of bleached yellow tape loosely covering a half-held door. A further handful of crying squeaks rang out as I walked towards it, years of ash being pushed from between cracks in the floor. The tape took no persuading at all to delicately fall to the ground. Beside the door, now visible underneath a film of dust, was the a plaque that read "ADMINISTRATION."

The door took little effort to breach, two of its three hinges were no longer even connected to it.

I reached for my flask as I looked around the dusty room. Half full, and soon empty, the container was hidden away in my pocket as I breathed in the smell of ominous decay. In this case that meant burnt wood and an overpowering smell of mold.

The feeling of retracing grew stronger as It drew my attention towards a set of filing cabinets. There were three in total, two leaned over each other like a small line of dominoes that had been gently toppled over. One laid face down on the floor, it's drawers pinned shut. Even from across the room there was a dull luster visible, the two visible cabinets had a rectangular label about the face. Creeping towards them, a small rodent leapt up and darted from the room. The first cabinet's label was covered in an expected film of dust. Wiping it off left a black smudge on a my right thumb, one that I instinctively rubbed on my right pant leg. I cursed myself in the dark, already able to make out what was clearly a new mold stain on my nice pants. Turning back to the cabinet, beneath the mold spores was a metal plaque that read "A-CG."

Somehow it didn't feel right.

The label on the cabinet beside it, when wiped, read "CH-F."

Still not right.

I looked down at the cabinet laying face down and my stomach filled with butterflies. I attempted to flip it up-right again and was met with a clattering cacophony as the drawers fell to the floor. Luckily the sudden reduction in weight made it much easier to right the cabinet itself. A mess of folders was now at my feet, as well as the now half empty drawers. Wiping off the label of the cabinet revealed a much more corroded "P-S"

One drawer did remain at the top, a sliding lock held it in place. Unlocking it, I slid it open. Inside was a series of even more folders, better kept and still arranged alphabetically. Combing through them, a jolt ran through my hand as I reached a folder with a label almost too worn to read.

Almost.

Opening it, the world went dim and seemed to fade away again.

XIX

It is frightening, how things can seem so hopeless and yet fall into place so effortlessly. If not in the moment, it will most certainly appear as such in hindsight. Maybe that is a coping mechanism for dealing with reality. Of the few people I have spoken with, gotten to know, and then committed to memory, there seem to be two binary outcomes to self understanding: A whole and complete acceptance of the facts, and an entire lack thereof. I struggle to categorize my worldview as either. Neither denial nor acceptance have ever delivered me from grief.

...

There was a bright flash as my head thudded against the wall. I had woken myself up, or perhaps the weather had done that. Sheets of rain battered the window of my bedroom. There was the sound of thunder, a similar deep thrum as the thump that had awoken me. It was storming still, the lights were off, and my head hurt terribly.

It was another incident of teleportation then; I'd arrived home with no immediate knowledge of how. I looked out the window to try and gauge the time and was met with soft rainy daylight.

I groaned, "Aaaagghhh."

My mouth seemed to stick to itself as I concluded the outcry. My eyes were as dry as my mouth. My bones felt heavy yet brittle. My muscles were sore. I heaved myself out of the bed and struggled towards the light switch, only to think better of it and walk into the kitchen instead. The soft stormy light guided me through the windows, finer details of my home were sometimes briefly illuminated in the bright flashes of lightening.

"The darkness will hold me, the darkness will warm my brittle bones today," I whispered to myself as I tramped hobbled towards the sink. With a turn of a knob, a stream of life giving water poured from the spigot. I craned my neck to wet my cracked lips, then the phone rang.

With a few large gulps of water in my stomach, I rushed towards the set and cleared my throat to answer, "Hello?"

"Simon!"

It was Marcus, "I was only calling to make sure you were alright. You looked terrible when you dropped off the portrait. I will be at your building tonight, I can't wait to see you again! Do you still have those supplies?"

"What? What supplies? The portrait? You found it?"

"YOU FOUND IT! And the diamonds, you *will* earn your money back on them my friend, we both will."

"The diamonds? On the skirt and in the eyes? Elsewhere? It was finished?"

"Brother, why are you asking me these questions? Are you getting things from someone else? I can't have any of that, you better be straight as an arrow with an empty pallette for tonight! I will see you at eight."

There was a click as the line went dead. A boon shook the apartment. I ran back to the sink and satiated the remainder of my thirst, and began a pot of coffee. The coffee maker politely blinked at me, it was six twenty pm. The world seemed to steady as the water reached my stomach and began to distribute itself around my body and into my brain. They couldn't have rescheduled the auction, but I couldn't have been away for a week. That wasn't something that could be dismissed by a bender or too deep a sleep. Rachel could've been halfway across the world by now if she so wished, and as far as I knew all I'd done is finish a picture of her. A picture that she seemed very uncomfortable with as time went on.

The coffee maker bubbled and gurgled and my stomach growled. I had to talk to her, but first I had to hear her voice. I looked towards the answering machine and expected to see a dead LCD. Instead I was greeted by a white box brightly displaying a bright back-lit "1" on its front. I crept towards the thing and pressed the black play button.

A robotic voice answered me, "One new message,"

It was followed by Marcus' voice, "Simon, I'm so glad I can reliably leave you messages now. You are welcome by the way! I need *A* portrait by tomorrow. Call me back!"

There was a beep and then the room was quiet again.

My old answering machine was gone. Rachel's note was gone.

"...Polimony?"

My eyes darted about, but there was no answer. I attempted to retrieve Rachel's number from memory and was successful, dialing the digits as they came to mind. The other end rung. Then it rang more. It continued to ring, until finally her voicemail was reached. Odd, but another attempt was made nonetheless. The same outcome was met.

Maybe I was biting off more than I could chew, I had only just woken up after all. I walked back to the happy coffee maker. It was always sad until I touched it, then a pot of coffee would appear and then I would be happy soon after. This time, as I poured a cup of coffee, I was not happy. I looked at the little numbers blink as I sipped at the warm liquid. Six thirty pm. Things seemed to move faster and faster, in an hour and a half I would be on the way to an auction that I had no business or interest being at.

But that was the least of my actual worries. Rachel had more than likely left town, leaving me in the process. Her note was gone, and with it was any hope of figuring out how to keep her. My throat began to close, only this time it had nothing to do with dehydration.

There was an odd air about the apartment. It was empty, and as I mindlessly reached for the liquor cabinet, the choking sensation only worsened. That was the problem, I was the problem. And now, for the time being, there was only me. There was no art, there was no bickering, there was no romance. There was no distraction from the feeling that had been clawing at me all along. Was this purgatory? Would an hour and a half last an eternity? I pondered on these thoughts and spiked the brown bile with clear respite.

Half and half wasn't a great breakfast, but it satisfied me just the same.

The phone rang again, and I broke from my mood and picked it up in a desperate craze, "What? What is it? Who is this?"

"Simon it's Marcus. I knew you would be whetting your appetite, you fiend! This is why I will be there in a few minutes. I cannot have you out of service for tonight."

"Oh..."

"Don't sound so disappointed, I have better things anyways. The usual and more."

"Well,"

"Well nothing. I will be there soon, come downstairs and have fun with me before we make some money."

"Oh, well okay."

"Perfect."

And then the line went dead.

It was unreal. The only genuine thing that failed to confuse or frighten me was the lukewarm mixture between both my hands. The pitter-patter of rain drops continued as I prepared then hurried downstairs.

An old stretch was parked out front. The engine was humming and a faceless man stood by a lowered window.

The smell of liquor and herbs wafted out of the limousine as Marcus spoke "Simon, you stress too much. I can see it on your face. Get in the car."

Hinges squeaked as the gaunt figure opened a wide black door for me.

The body of the long vehicle swayed smoothly as I sat in the cabin. The interior was a deep purple and lit by an uncountable amount of bulbs. There was indeed a mini bar, as promised over the phone.

"I've had a lot happen in the past couple weeks Mark, I think I've got good reasons to be stressed. I've been blacking out, it's ridiculous."

There was a thud as the door was shut behind me. "Simone, have a drink,"

"You know I hate that, 'Simone.'"

"It is only a joke. Here," Marcus grabbed a glass from the hideaway compartment. The otherwise seamless interior of the stretch was interrupted only by two odd panel gaps. Before Marcus could close it, I was able to see an unreasonably many questionable things. It was an odd limo, clearly retrofitted repeatedly over time.

The glass that my old friend had grabbed was no full of dark liquid and passed towards me.

A bump made the contents shake as I held it tightly, careful not to spill what was inside. I tried to slam the contents, spilling about half of it on my shirt in the process. Before I could apologize, another glass was handed to me – full.

"Really?"

Marcus nodded his head, "Whatever you have going on, I'd like you to forget about it for a night."

"It isn't that simple, what if Rachel's gone?"

"She will be there! On a canvas! Do you not see how silly you sound my friend?"

"That isn't what I meant, she said she'd have to leave town, and she didn't answer her phone tonight."

There was another bump as Marcus shut his eyes and seemed to finally understand the depth of the situation.

"One night Simon. Give me one night."

"What the heck is wrong with you?"

"At least give it a chance. You look like shit, and it doesn't sound like it's for a fun reason."

I thought on that for a moment then slammed back a second drink. He was right for once.

XX

You aren't a product of those you surround yourself with, you are an average.

Though averages tend to be rougher when you only have a few people in your life.

...

A thousand stimuli, through a mere five senses, flooded into my consciousness. The bombardment of traffic sounds and mixed sources of light was enough to wake me, not yet considering everything else. As I postured myself, there was a deep thud as my head hit a ceiling. The ceiling was much lower than expected. Rubbing my eyes, partially obscured street lights came into view. A pair of lights would come and go, disappearing into the black void that the rest of the bokeh leapt from. They were cars, similar to the one that I was clearly inside of. My vision cleared as I restrained myself from further eye-rubbing. The cabin of this vehicle was long and purple. It was a limousine. I was in the back of *the* limousine. To my right was a brick building with sporadically spaced out pillars. I was inside of an unattended limo, parked outside of the downtown gallery and auction house.

This had become absurd. I was losing enough time that it had become a question whether it even mattered anymore.

There was a rap at the window beside me, the noise rattled along the interior.

A muffled voice made its way through the tinted glass as I searched for the roller.

The voice became clearer as I began to lower window.

It was Marcus' voice, "... Five minutes, and then several, and then a dozen, and now you ignore – Ah, Simon. Finally back for your big night."

I leaned my head out of the limo and sucked in as much cool night air as possible.

Marcus laughed, "What the hell happened? Can't handle sedatives anymore?"

"Sedatives?"

"Well you looked awfully wound up earlier. Welcome back! You really had me worried, not that anyone ever dies from that stuff. What took you so long anyways?"

My words came out slowly, each one requiring an uncomfortable amount of effort to vocalize, "What are you talking about? When did I take sedatives?"

"In the drink!"

"Why the hell would you –"

"Simon, everything is fine now. And your number is almost up, for G-d's sake get out of the car."

I opened the passenger side door and reeled out, an absolute lump of flesh and sweat. It was at this point I realized how incapacitated I was. "I'm really slated to be up soon?"

"Soon enough, there is a piece they are calling 'Farmer's eyes' being shown right now. I heard somebody yawn when it arrived, though that may have been me. The penny people will have a go over it."

My legs straightened one muscle at a time as I tried to shake some alertness into myself.

"Did Rachel make it?"

"Of course, I told you she'll be up at any moment."

"No, *Rachel*, as in the subject of the piece."

Marcus laughed again, "You sound ridiculous. Here, take this."

He handed me a white tablet.

I frowned while palming its smooth exterior. "Why?"

"You sound so sad to receive a gift. It is only from the chemist, my friend. No more surprises."

I continued to stare at the little thing, for some reason unable to conjure any thoughts about it or anything else.

Marcus continued, "It will wake you up a bit so you don't sound so silly. Now shut that door and make sure to chew it. I bought the peppermint ones!"

There was a satisfying clunk as I shut the limo door. The round white tablet did indeed taste minty. The flavor stayed agreeable with each crunch between the jaws. It could've been a breath mint to me if it weren't for the hint of salt. Water splashed as my left shoe encountered a deep puddle. There was an atmosphere to the night. It was an atmosphere of jubilance and consumption that defied the dank darkness of the otherwise open city streets. I craned my still aching neck to allow a better view of the building before me. Red brick and gray mortar made up a large portion of the exterior, the pillars of white marble in front of it supported nothing structural. Rather, they supported an air of authority presumably held by the structure they guarded. In this case it was an authority over what was valued. It was pompous and often pretentious, but at times it provided income to myself and others. A step here and a step there, within a short while the walk to the entrance was over. Two double doors, made of mahogany and perhaps imported. My likeness, verified dually by plastic and paper.

Upon entering the antechamber before the main hall, it was evident that something was garnering more than enough warring bids. A single voice commanded the figures as the odd sign was raised and then quietly lowered.

"One thousand."

"Two thousand."

Within half a minute, the bid had surpassed five thousand dollars.

I grinned at the display, "Why, I'm doing very well."

Marcus slunk behind me, "Simon, that isn't yours."

"Oh."

The bidding continued, before culminating in a final series of half-statements made by the auctioneer.

"Eleven-thousand one-hundred and eighty dollars. Going once. Going twice."

There was a satisfying thump followed by an exciting conclusion,

"Right-o, sold to number one zero eight. Now for lot number eighteen, 'Rebirth in E.'"

I looked around and couldn't see Rachel anywhere. The few spread out bodies in the antechamber were easy to scan through, but it seemed that most everybody was in the main chamber where the auction was being properly held. Despite the lack of contact, I still hoped that she would be here. For some reason, a more rational side of myself was slowly taking over.

I turned towards my friend, suddenly keen on how lucid he was, "Mark, have you heard from her at all? Have you seen Rachel in any way at all? Is she here or not?"

"Who?"

"Rachel. Rachel Rachel Rachel."

"Ah. Like I said, she is number thirty-seven my friend! Many more for us to look at, and maybe even bid on, between this one and that."

The painting. He was still talking about that damned painting. "No, the human being, the woman, the subject, Rachel!"

Marcus shrugged and gestured to his left. Following his hands, there was another threshold leading to a laminated counter. There were various bottles behind it, all guarded by an aging bald man. The bald one wiped a glass and looked at nothing in particular. As he turned this way and that, the light reflecting off his head revealed how incredibly polished and shiny it was.

I shook my head, "I'm not in the mood for a drink, I need to find a phone."

A bright heat radiated from my stomach.

Marcus smiled as I winced at the sensation, "You should get water. Those tablets can be hard on the bowels."

I shadowed Marcus as he led me through the wide entryway. The bar was quite large despite half of it being under apparent construction. The functioning half was sparsely populated with slow moving figures.

My bottom found the top of an uncomfortable wooden stool. "A water would help, and maybe he has lemons too. But only water, I don't think I have a lot of money with me."

Marcus chuckled, "The bar is open!"

"I can see that."

"No, FREE."

"Is that why we're here and not across the street?"

There was an audible gasp in the auction hall as another, undoubtedly better, piece was unveiled.

The bald one looked up and rushed towards us, almost knocking over a cute pyramid of glasses on the way.

"Apologies gentlemen, there are some renovations under way. Even the usual furniture is out of commission while it is re-stained, re-sealed, and re-upholstered."

He palmed two glasses from the top of the pyramid and filled them with water, both the solid and liquid, then slid them in front of Marcus and I. I removed my coat and placed it on the back of my chair, a feverish warmth had begun to set itself upon me.

Marcus shuffled his water towards me and bumped my elbow, "Two neat vodkas please."

I tried my best to appear as weary as I felt, eyeing Marcus until he noticed.

"... Both in one glass, if that is okay."

Without any hesitation, the bald one nodded and eyeballed a double shot of vodka. In the split second he turned around to do it, a glare from the lights bounced off his perfectly polished crown and blinded me. I squeezed my eyes shut as Marcus set down a now empty glass. He had apparently been just as quick in drinking it.

A fact suddenly occurred to me while I massaged my head, "Mark, you have a cellphone! Could I use it?"

"Ha ha ha. No!"

I almost knocked over the waters, "What? Why"

"Because I don't have it! Why would I risk somebody interrupting our fun? This is business *and* pleasure. I am in no need of a potential addition to what is already complete. Thus, I have happily severed myself from the possibility."

I paused for a moment, momentarily unsure of what to say. He had made a fair point. "Surely there is a payphone here? Do you think the bar has a phone?"

The bald one answered from across the counter, "It's cut off at the moment. It hasn't worked for a couple hours now. Maybe longer."

"Then a payphone?"

"Down the street maybe –"

There was a deep sniff as Marcus quickly indulged himself and spoke, "Simon, is this not more important than your latest fling? There is always another. I understand that you have not heard from this Rachel in a while. Perhaps your recent encounter with her was not as pleasant as expected, and perhaps it was even the last. But her image, her perfect form, the ideal being that only you could translate into a medium rivaling that of flesh, that is here. That will always be yours, even after it is sold here tonight."

I dwelt within his words for a time. Even if they were partially the product of indulgence and hedonistic consumption, they were also a partial product of truth.

"She isn't here Mark. And that image isn't hers. It isn't mine. And soon it won't be yours either."

Marcus cleared his throat and turned again towards the bald one, "Another two vodkas please."

The man nodded his head, and I averted my gaze as went back to work.

Turning back to me, Marcus looked this way and that before reaching into his pocked and handing me a coin. He paused, and then handed me a second coin as well. "Two calls. Never has a woman possessed you like *this*. Rarely has a woman occupied your mind for more than a *week*. For that, I offer my condolences. But only two calls. It is for your health. I hope that her voice, be it actual or prerecorded, will bring you peace. At least for tonight.

There was a deep lurch in my stomach as I pocketed the coins. The ill feeling was followed by another as the bald one slid a freshly filled glass towards Marcus, hiding away the old one before my old friend could push it away.

I asked the man, "What street was that payphone on?"

"For Christ's sake, any street. We're downtown, hook a left when you walk out and keep walking."

That last word hung in the air above him, illuminated by the reflection of his incredibly smooth scalp. There was always so much walking.

Before I could fully stand, the bald one spoke again, "Don't forget your coat. There's a cold snap tonight and you look like shit."

Marcus drained the vodka and sunk into the awkward bar chair. It looked deeply uncomfortable a position, and yet he seemed as comfortable as could be.

"Mark, I'll be back in a few. You said we've got time before *Rachel* is shown?"

"Sure buddy, a lot of time."

As I headed out, I heard a crash followed by the bald one's voice, "The door stays OPEN!"

The antechamber towards the exit was even emptier than before, a hint that perhaps I was missing out on something. It didn't matter though, nothing else mattered. The ache in my stomach seemed to a settle settle a bit. Looking to my left, there was a row of streetlights with fenced trees in between. Businesses and row homes stood opposite both sides, a narrow road between them. This was the place I'd chosen as a home. This carved environment where the theater of my life was to play out for the time being. Thoughts like these cycled through my head like a never ending slot machine. There was a payout to be made, if not to me then to someone else. It was cold, the air hung about, and there was an odd smell of charcoal. I walked away from all of it, towards a tall blue box at the end of the block. The sound of sirens echoed from further away. Too far to discern if they were police or an ambulance. The odd passerby was still present, wading about the muck towards nothing. Luckily, the phone booth was empty. I hung my coat on an interior hook and fumbled in my pockets for the coins. One coin lighter, I picked up the dusty receiver and waited for the tone. Then, I dialed Rachel's number.

...

...

...

"Hey, this is Rachel. You missed me but feel free to leave a mess–"
I hung up. The second coin evaded my grasp until finally succumbing to my desperate reach. A part of me knew she wouldn't pick up, but I wanted to hear her voice again. Marcus was right, her voicemail alone made everything in the world stand still for a while. Even if it only lasted until the beep. I released the second coin and tried once more.

The line rung again.

And again.

Then something extraordinary happened.

It stopped ringing.

There was an ambient sound on the other end, the sound of slow breathing followed by fumbling until finally the line went dead.

I would have rather heard her voicemail.

XXI

You aren't a product of those you surround yourself with, you're an average.

That average tends to get rougher and rougher the fewer and fewer you put towards it.

What are you when you're alone?

...

When I returned to the bar, Marcus was still there. A pile of glasses had grown beside him. "Simon! My friend, my buddy, how are you?"

It was immediately apparent that he had emptied them all.

"Marcus, I need to talk to you, has my piece come up yet?"

The bald one interrupted me, "No. They're at thirty-one right now. Thirty-seven right?"

I looked at Marcus and he nodded his head.

"You've got time. I cut your friend off, but I caught the number from him during his... *musings*. Where is he from anyways?"

Marcus sobered and turned to better face the bald one, "I am a native of this place! Leave that out of it!"

The man just stared at him.

I looked at my friend and then at the man, "He's fine, better than me actually. Could I have a neat shot of gin? And do you have any coffee?"

The man laughed, "You must hate yourself or something. Do you mind old coffee?"

I shook my head.

"Of course you don't. Give me a moment, one to one right? What kind of gin do you want?"

"No preference."

As the bald one prepared my half and half, I turned towards my addled friend. "Mark, you greedy fuck."

Marcus smiled, a devilish grin that only substance could allow. "I gave you one on the way here. You slept it off remember? In a few hours, I will be fine... Did he say thirty-one? We need to go, or... I will miss our great return..."

He seemed to contemplate the last statement, momentarily unaware of his surroundings. Reality reentered his eyes and he looked down at himself, "I may have over indulged."

The bald one returned with a glass of dark liquid, and a second slightly taller glass of hopefully water. "Good luck with that one."

I sipped at it and pondered what to do about Marcus. The bald one began to turn away but I suddenly had the vigor to ask, "Wait, wait don't turn around please. Why are you so bald?"

He laughed, "What kind of question is that? I'm sixty-two years old."

"No, there is no possible way a man that old could have such a shiny and tight scalp."

The bald one laughed again and proceeded to turn from us anyways, "I moisturize!"

I was unable to avert my gaze in time as a stray beam once again filled my sight with domed light.

When I was able to see again, he was chuckling by another group that had just sat down. It didn't matter, looking at Marcus again it was obvious we'd both had enough. I sipped again at the bitter drink, each sip seemed to erase the events of fifteen minutes ago.

Marcus, even in his useless state, finally picked up on my troubles. "Simon, you look unhappy."

It was enough to make me laugh, "That is a fair observation."

"Do you want to be here tonight?"

"I just wanted to see her."

"Well –"

"IN THE FLESH."

Marcus smiled, the same wide grin of substance as before, "Then why don't we."

"What are you on about? What happened to this being 'our night' ?"

"I said I wanted 'our night' to be fun. I have drugged you, I have drugged myself, and still we are not having fun. *You* are not having fun."

I looked down into my almost empty glass, unsure of whether I wanted to finish it or not. Whatever the white tablet had done, the drink was slowly undoing.

Marcus tapped me and began to whisper, "You stay to see what *Rachel* sells for, and then I get our driver to take us to her home."

He said it as though it were a secret plan, then he quickly shouted, "Where is that driver anyways? Is he looking at the art?"

A man with gray peppered hair raised his hand from across the bar, "waiting on the call, sir."

I narrowed my eyes to see him, noticing a tall glass in front of him, "You're drinking then? Before driving us?"

He tapped the glass and chuckled, "all virgins for me, as usual."

the latter half of his sentence was concluded with a devilish grin, though not one of substance.

It was of something much worse.

At least that kind of disposition doesn't impair driving.

I almost leapt from my seat.

What? Do I scare you now?

Polimony had appeared in the chair next to me.

"Mark friend, I need to use the bathroom."

Marcus stared at the bar top and slowly nodded his head, "Those pill will do that to you. I will be near the back of the auction hall. I need to gather myself.. Is all..."

He was absolutely lost in whatever he had indulged in. There was a fix for that though, often in one of his pockets.

I reached for my glass and finally finished it. The bitter mixture jolted me a bit before warming me.

It had grown significantly colder outside. I didn't need to use the bathroom, that had been a lie.

You're getting good at that.

"Good at what?"

At lying.

Her blonde hair made my heart melt but her presence froze it in place.

"Believe it or not, I don't want you here right now."

I do believe you. Plus, I helped with this painting didn't I? I want to see how people react to our work.

I reached for my head, considering the situation of the portrait in quiet.

Polimony dragged her fingers across the sleeve of my coat as she walked around me.

Can't I be around you for a while? In the same room even?

"I wanted a break, a short pause while I situate things. I'm having a lot of trouble right now..."

Break? Pause? You act like I simply disappear. We've been over this, you know that isn't the case. I get bored..."

She stroked my sleeve and again and stopped beside me,

I get lonely...

The endless internal conflict grew again, within me. "You said you wouldn't do anything."

Now she was in front of me, visibly annoyed.

What? I can't help? I can't joke around? I do in fact get bored waiting for you. It isn't always about Simon. Can you at least concede to that?

And then it snapped. All that was left inside was something broken. It didn't matter.

"You're right."

I'm right?

"I haven't been considerate, but if you haven't noticed: Rachel isn't here. That bothers me. When I go to call her, she either doesn't pick up or she does something really creepy and hangs up. That really bothers me. I'm out in the cold arguing with you. That also bothers me. I"m stuck at an auction that, at this point, I don't really care much about. That bothers me as well. I'm sorry I haven't spent any time with you, or called your name, at even communicated this. It's just beginning to feel like a bit too much for me."

Polimony's expression softened.

You're going to love what I've done for us Simon. She's exactly the way you always wanted her... I love you.

And then she vanished. She simply ceased to be. Of course, I knew better than that. She hadn't literally vanished, only visibly and audibly. Thinking back in the present moment, this meant very little. The only grace to her departure was that I could again sift through some personal errands undisturbed. At least, for the time being.

More people had entered that initial antechamber, though not enough to make me feel that I was too late. The two doors to the auction hall were partially opened, and I did my best to quietly weasel between them. Marcus was almost immediately on the other side, and quickly pulled me towards him. His eyes were wide and clearer than before.

His hot breath whispered violently in my ear, "I am so happy to see you my friend! You have arrived almost right on queue!"

I grimaced as his sudden enthusiasm moistened my inner ear, "Good Lord Mark, are you going to hoard everything tonight?"

Marcus reached into his pocket, "Here? Really? I like this shiny new bold Simon, in fact, I love him!"

I softly held his arm in place and matched his aggressive whispering, "NO! In fact, never mind. I am not in the mood. We can't do that in the middle of these people!"

Several coughs could be heard, as a handful of cast glares landed on us both.

Marcus finally caught the hint, "Oh, yes... That makes sense."

A young man of dark complexion was behind a podium at center stage. To his left, a platform with a covered canvas was wheeled beside him.

He cleared his throat as two classily dressed women removed the cover, "That brings us to number thirty-six: 'Our Descent'"

The removal revealed a dark stained canvas, glossy dark tones reflecting light in various textures, patches of indescribable forms. What was almost describable was the feeling it brought: a feeling of losing things piece by piece. Of dying but never being dead. Maybe this was something worth attending.

"We will start the bidding at eleven hundred."

A sign rose up, and fell when acknowledged. This continued on for several cycles until a final price was reached.

"...Forty-five-hundred, going once, going twice... SOLD to bidder one-forty-two"

The piece was covered once more by the two women and wheeled away. There was a brief pause as people spoke among themselves and the auction host wrote something down. I could feel Marcus fidgeting beside me.

"Simon, that last one was painful, but in a wonderful way. I wish it had come after yours, that way I could confidently bid on it."

"Why not just commission me? I can make two."

He shook his head, "Even you must admit that they could never be completely identical."

"Isn't that the beauty in it?"

Marcus grabbed his chin, and pondered this as the auction host cleared his throat once more. The two women returned, this time, with a covered item that looked exactly the same size as 'Rachel'.

"This next piece is a work by someone thought to be retired. Number thirty-seven... 'Rachel'"

The women removed the cover once more.

"Bidding has been set to start at... three thousand."

I almost threw up again, "Mark, what the hell?"

He seemed bothered as well, "Yes, what in the hell indeed my friend. He should have said 'thirty thousand'... It will reach the target though, I have a special surprise for you."

I shook my head, "That is NOT what bothered me about that announcement. It's finished, the dust, you didn't just find it, you finished it."

Marcus looked confused as a sign shot up. And then another. And another. And it continued, until finally it didn't anymore. "Twenty-nine thousand, five-hundred, going once, going twice, SOLD to bidder two-eighteen."

Marcus scowled, "Thirty thousand, thirty thousand, the greedy bastards..."

I turned to him, torn between great surprise and great bewilderment, "The diamond dust, the blending. It's finished. How did you know to do all of that?"

He tilted his head, "You found it Simon, and you seemed quite proud to have finished it when you brought it to me."

XXII

How can it seem that nobody knows about something so obvious? It's absurd. Almost as absurd about a single person not knowing something that everyone else seems to know.

…

"I have to go."

Marcus appeared suddenly unhappy, "Already?"

"I don't know. The Rachel thing was on my mind, but this is too much."

"Ha ha, are you playing a joke on me? This is everything you wanted."

"I wanted too much then."

"Do you need to be satisfied this badly, that you cannot even enjoy a success?"

"It isn't a success. It's just another act."

The sides of his mouth tightened, he was smiling a sinister grin devoid of happiness, "Fine, I will grab the driver and we will go to her building, if only to finish this so you can move on. She is nearby anyways? You said she lives downtown?"

It was amazing what indulgence in substance could do to someone.

"No, Mark, she lives on South 46th."

"You act like this is far!"

By now the energy from before had escaped the room, to make space for other art pieces.

"It's on the other side of town."

"The other side of *down*-town."

"That's kind of a leap don't you think?"

"A leap is nothing when you have a car! Does your subject partake?"

I held my hand out flat and wiggled it a bit, that was to say: "a little."

170

The antechamber had filled back up slightly, and nobody made room for our obvious haste. It was odd; despite the weight my name still held, nobody recognized me.

"You have lost weight Simone."

"Don't call me that."

"Alright, alright. But you do look much different, old friend. Were it not for the constant visits, I may have been oblivious as well."

The driver took a heavy turn and the contents of the cabin lurched to my left.

Marcus balled up his fist and knocked it against the divider, "Aye!"

A muffled apology snuck its way through as the vehicle steadied.

"You told him to drive quickly"

"And I told him to keep my buzz in mind. 'No substance in the car' and yet he will drive away my spirits like he is spiting me. Is he spiting me Simon?"

"No, and it might be for the best. You've been awfully greedy with it."

"You didn't want any!"

"Pour me another drink."

"Hypocrite, the bottle is almost empty."

"There are more."

The limousine swerved again, this time less dramatically.

Marcus glared at the divider, "That, I can at least tolerate. You did not tell me that she lived in the third ward."

"Yes, I did. And I said she lived on South 46th, *near* the third ward."

"No no, she lives *in* the third ward. South 46th is *in* the third ward. Are we at least close?"

The question didn't seem directed at me, but I looked out the window anyway. A sign addressing South 35th flew by.

I flicked my glass as Marcus rummaged for a different bottle, "We are on 35th, it's close enough."

He finally found one, most likely one of his cheaper ones, and began slowly pouring it into my glass.

He peered out of his window as he poured it, "This area bothers me."

"It's fine, we are in a nice car."

The limo continued on a straight course as Marcus stowed the bottle, "Yes, the reason that it bothers me."

South 40th shot by, followed by a slowly passing South 42nd. The divider began to slowly fall and the back of our drivers head was quickly replaced by the side of his face as the vehicle made a right.

The driver sounded enthusiastically gruff as we gradually met the speed limit. "What street number did you say?"

Marcus cut me off before I could speak, "Did I push the G-d damned button!?"

I gave Marcus an angry and answered before the divider rose, "6000."

"Thanks..."

The divider rose up, seemingly faster; as impossible as that could've been.

I cleared my throat between sips of liquor, "for G-d's sake, he only wants to get us there."

My friend breathed deeply, then exhaled, "I apologize Simon. That was rude of me."

This was followed by the same wicked smile that did little to assuage me.

There was the sounds of sirens, louder and then quickly quieter.

Marcus smiled wider, "See, this is why I do not like places like this. Always the sirens, this way and that. I would only come to a place like this for you, dear dear friend."

As the car came to a stop, only the outline of the building was visible through the deep tint of the limousine. It was odd, the shape of the place. I rolled the window down to get better sight of it.

Marcus jumped through the new opening and sucked in a deep lungful of cool night air, "Oh, oh my... What floor did she live on Simon?"

Half of the seventh floor appeared entirely black, even in the moon light. Yellow streamers danced in the gentle breeze, even from here it was obvious what they were.

"The seventh."

It could've been some weird power outage if it weren't for all the lit windows around it. They dimly illuminated the reality of what most likely happened.

"...four, five, six... Which part of the seventh?"

The darkest spot, obvious source, flooded me with panic and an odd sense of weightlessness.

Marcus noticed me ignoring him and turned around to face me. He reached for the roller but I stopped him. "I hope she isn't home."

There was a lurch as Marcus slunk back to his side of the cabin, "Why?"

I reached for the divider button in a successful attempt at lowering it. "Please, drive away from here."

The driver nodded, not even asking for a destination.

Marcus pressed the divider button repeatedly in an equally successful attempt at raising it, "I thought you wanted to see her? What was this all about?"

"I think someone tried to burn her building down."

"What are you talking about?"

"Did you not see that half of her floor is just a dark charred blotch? The caution tape?"

Marcus shrugged his shoulders and pulled a straw from his pocket.

"Such is life in the third ward. You have to admit, it is still probably the nicest building for several blocks."

"Mark, what is wrong with you? I think my girlfriend might be in serious trouble."

There was a great exchange of air and substance before he responded, "You are overreacting. I'm sure they evacuated before it was put out. It is a brick building, I would wager it has dozens of fires. Mordechai lives near here too, his building had three fires last month. He only noticed one of them, and that was the one *he* started."

"Mordechai?"

"Yes, the one that loves stovetop popcorn and sleeping pills."

"Who in the world is Mordechai?"

"The driver!"

"Fuck, it doesn't matter anyways. She won't answer her phone, her portion of the building is all crisped up -"

"- And full of flavor!"

"- And full of details! Secrets! Bad energy and maybe her body!"

"It is standard practice to remove those, Simon."

I looked at Marcus as he wildly began to rummage for a bottle in the middle of our conversation. The divider sunk again. The racket of clinking glass stopped as my old friend noticed, "What the hell?"

"I pressed the button, Mordechai? Mordechai. Could you take us to South 7th and Main?"

There was no verbal response, but the vehicle took a hard left and the divider rose.

Marcus seemed momentarily sobered, "seventh and main?"

I nodded, "I've got to be home."

XXIII

It hardly mattered one bit where one thing went or another. Everything in the world ought to end up in the same place.

...

There were the same pair of eyes looking into mine as before. The same blue eyes I'd become accustomed to.

Hi!

"Leave me alone."

Why do you sound like that?

A stray beam of light snuck between the blinds and struck my right eye. I quickly rolled over into darkness.

I thought last night went really well.

There were a series of nudges against my lower back. Soon, then rose to my upper back. Eventually, I was being assaulted, and couldn't bear it anymore.

"For G-d's sake Polimony, if you were able to displace me I'd be atoms by now. Why can't I mourn in peace?"

Mourn what?

"This is exactly why. Nobody cares. Nobody seems to even notice."

She isn't irreplaceable

I shot out of bed, "That! That right there! What has gotten into you? What lacking has caused this apathy. Her home is gone, I still haven't even seen it in the news!"

These things happen.

"These things happen, yeah. And I'm just left to my own devices."

It isn't like she was the last woman on Earth, sometimes people don't call back.

"Polimony, there is a hole where her apartment used to be. How is this not registering with anybody!?"

By now I'd become animated, awakened, fully lucid.

Polimony was as she always was.

What's wrong?

"You really don't care."

About what?

"About a potential fatality, the death of someone I loved."

We had an agreement. She left. And you are re-negging. That's unfair.

"I'm? I'm being unfair?"

Polimony seemed to float towards the kitchen, so casual in her movements.

Yes.

I followed her at once, annoyed to find a great many new things in the space.

"What is all of this?"

You earned quite a bit from that auction. That woman just about renovated our entire apartment!

"Why would I want that?"

There was a new couch.

"When?"

There was new tile.

"She's splattered about the entire place."

There were works, hung, leveled, framed.

"Her remains cover every nook and cranny."

A new coffee maker chimed, a soft 'toot' followed by the smell of cappuccino.

Why do you look so upset?

Why don't you wake up?

Simon?

Why don't you wake up?

"AAAA!"

And so it was, I was back in bed again. Only this time, everything was just the same.

Polimony churned about beside me,

What's gotten into you.

I looked around again, I even leapt from the bed and inspected the kitchen and the living area. There was nothing new. Same crappy furniture and bland walls. Same crappy coffee maker.

"I had a terrible nightmare."

Polimony slunk behind me. Dreary morning light leaked in through the blinds.

Was it about Rachel?

I looked at my muse for a moment before responding, "Yeah, in a way it was about everything *but*."

That's interesting. Have you put any thought towards our arrangement, seeing as she hasn't called?

There was a dainty quality to Polimony's eyelashes. She even blinked along with her last couple of syllables to emphasize it.

Well?

"What is wrong with you, am I still dreaming?"

Am I that wonderful this morning?

"No. I had a nightmare where you spent all of our recent income on frivolous objects."

I don't see how I could do that, or why I would want to.

"It's beside the point, it isn't as though my relationship with Rachel has decayed. If she dies -"

- If she dies, I consider it an Act..

"- Ah, yes. But suppose it was another person who killed her, not some grand event -"

What are you getting at?

"Her apartment burned down, doesn't that seem odd? She showed us so many pictures of people doing the same exact thing to people like her, people like us!"

And you are surprised that it happened to her?

"Well. no... But it is still very worrisome. I would be a broken man right now were it not for her probable foresight."

Yeah.

"Yeah?"

Yeah Simon. Just yeah. It doesn't have to mean anything else.

Polimony wound her way to the table and sunk into a chair. Thankfully, they were the same as before.

A thought suddenly came to mind.

"Polimony, how would you feel about a new couch?"

What? Why do you want a couch?

Maddening. I started a pot of coffee and reached for the liquor cupboard.

"I don't know. Just a thought."

The pot began to gurgle.

The cupboard was empty.

Are you going to paint again?

I looked at the small blonde apparition and for some odd reason felt it necessary to consider the events of my life up to this point. She was at the center of all of it.

"Yes. Very soon, in fact."

ACT V

XXIV

When you find the root of a weed you pull it. When the root of all your problems is inside of you, that only leaves one thing to do.

...

The cool autumn air had long since turned into that brisk sheer of the winter. It was fine though, any other time it would have been a bother but for now it was a much needed shock to the system. It felt as though it might snow, and yet the sky held out for now. I had put on a second coat anyways, something to shield me from the chance of exposure should the weather suddenly turn harsh. All of this I felt as I stepped off of the Mass Transit bus onto the colored cobbled stone of the Rainbow District. A set of soft footsteps clopped alongside me as Polimony caught up.

Sorry, I think I forgot to mention that I don't want to be here.

I continued toward Marcus' paint shop a bit slower, "You've mentioned it several times."

And yet...

"You could have stayed home."

A white flake drifted downward in front of me. It was soon joined by several more.

That would have been boring.

Yellow and black checkers skirted my peripheral vision, a taxi, gone as fast as it came.

"So you'd rather be uncomfortable than bored?"

Polimony leapt a couple feet in front of me to stand at the entrance of the shop.

Yes.

I put a hand through her abdomen and opened the door, a chime sounded as my muse wafted around me.

Marcus was at the counter stacking dominoes. Another chime sounded and was followed by a cascade of tinkling as the little rectangles clattered apart.

"Marcus! I need paint."

"Already? I love it, I love the sound of that! No more disappearing for Simone, only work!"

My teeth grinded on their own.

"Okay, *Simon*. Don't look so mad. What do you need?"

"Paint, I told you. I'm rushing this one, it just has to be completed."

"What happened to all that artsy talk? If all you need is paint, why come here? Why don't you have paint at home?"

"I need new paint, and new brushes. Everything has to be new."

Marcus put his hands up, "Alright alright, you have a system. Are you paying for this or are we splitting the sale?"

"Split sale, the portrait is yours once I'm done. I just need to complete it."

My old friend began rummaging about under the counter, "The way you are talking I do not know what to expect. Another portrait you said?"

He stood up with an assortment of generic brushes and a standard pallet of acrylic.

"Yeah, it's a portrait."

He placed them in a bag and went beneath the counter again, "See my friend, I told you. You are already onto the next one! How is she? When did you meet? What does she look like?"

This time he rose with a medium sized canvas, "Is this a good size? Do you need anything else?"

"It doesn't matter, that looks about right. This is all perfect. And about the subject... It's a surprise."

Marcus looked at all the boring art supplies on the counter and frowned, "She must not be that special."

I grabbed everything and looked at my muse.

"They might be the most special person I'll ever paint."

XXV

...

It was a rush job indeed. A basic outline, a basic color fill in. The skin tone matched, the hair color matched, a gray sweater and a black background. Possibly the worst thing I'd ever painted, and yet the most important. I tapped at a glass of gin beside me as I studied the finished portrait. I wasn't sure yet if it was the right thing to do but, given everything that had occurred, it felt right.

Polimony crept up beside me.

That's almost hurtful.

"It's the action that matters."

The portrait was already dry, having been made up in acrylic. The entire work took the better part of several hours.

You didn't get my nose right.

"Or the eyes, or the mouth, or the hair, you can stop anytime you know."

The work was set atop the kitchen table.

You're no fun.

I sipped at the glass and tapped it again. The circular ripples made for a wonderful momentary distraction.

Polimony poked my shoulder.

What's wrong with you?

I just continued to stare at the picture.

"I'm thinking."

I looked at the coffee maker clock. Marcus was meant to be here ten minutes ago.

About what?

There was a knock at the door.

"Come in Mark! It's unlocked."

I still don't see why you couldn't just bring it to him.

I held up a finger to my muse as Marcus slunk into the apartment.

"Simon! Already finished? You were not exaggerating when you said..."

He trailed off as he looked away from me and studied the portrait. The utterance that followed served to settle what few doubts remained within me: "Simone, you said you would never paint a self portrait."

I beamed as the recognition finally sank into all that were present. My muse seemed to lift from the paint.

It was done, there was nothing left to be said of the matter. I would have painted the entire world, if it could only bring back what had been lost.

In a way, that was exactly what I'd done.